"Masterful . . . a novel of survival and longing and love, and in many ways a modern portrait of an artist as a young man . . . a book written for *us,* I can hear so many people of so many different demographics say—we Iranian Americans whom you don't often hear about . . . Reading *I Will Greet the Sun Again,* you are not a voyeur—you are an accomplice, a keeper of secrets, a friend on this journey of relentless intensity."

—POROCHISTA KHAKPOUR, *The Washington Post*

"[A] heartbreaking debut . . . Khabushani writes movingly about K's queer coming-of-age and his burgeoning identity as a writer." —*The New York Times Book Review*

"Tender and gut-wrenching . . . a book of astonishing accomplishment and bravery . . . This book is a triumph, one that will help the next generation understand our specific American childhood—how it felt to grow up with broken immigrant parents and one foot still in Iran, sitting in front of a TV in a sad apartment complex, dreaming of the good life."

—DINA NAYERI, *The Guardian*

"A tale of diaspora that is as gutting as it is tender. . . . Every word, deft and unassuming, shatters."

—ANAHIT BEHR *kinny*

"Beautiful . . . Khabushani renders K's experiences in poignant vignettes that speak to the young boy's sensitivity as he dreams of a better, albeit uncertain future. This heartrending tale will stay with readers." —*Publishers Weekly* (starred review)

"Powerful . . . Relates a difficult coming-of-age tale with a focus on the physicality of male bodies, their vulnerability and resilience." —*Booklist*

"A heat map of longing, shame, and resilience." —*New York*

"Life-affirming . . . Khabushani is a talented writer." —*The Sunday Times* (U.K.)

"Haunting and poetic." —*San Francisco Chronicle*

"*I Will Greet The Sun Again* is a moving debut, teeming with desire and light, and quietly devastating. Khashayar J. Khabushani's voice keens and surprises, and at the center of the book we find K, tenderhearted, spirit glowing like a beacon." —JUSTIN TORRES, author of *We the Animals*

"Khabushani's debut novel, devoted to adolescence in all its glory and devastation, is a marvel. Reading it, I felt the thrill and joy of encountering a major writer at the beginning of his career." —MEGHA MAJUMDAR, author of *A Burning*

"Why wasn't *I Will Greet the Sun Again* around when I was ten, when I was twenty? This is a book I've dreamed of reading my whole life. How to mourn the loss of a country that has become unrecognizable while living across the world in one that doesn't recognize you? How to dismantle the brutal ways men teach each other to (not) love other men? What to do with the love you still feel, however guiltily, for those who treated you violently? I wish I'd had Khabushani's clarified language for these questions to guide me when I was young. Better late than never, Khashayar J. Khabushani. I am jealous of the generation of people who will grow up in a world with *I Will Greet the Sun Again* in it. I will be thinking about these characters forever." —KAVEH AKBAR, author of *Martyr!*

"A story for us brown kids who grew up in apartment complexes, making our own breakfast, lunch, and dinner because our immigrant parents were away at work . . . Khabushani's voice is a revelation; he has written a novel that shows what it means to grow up into a beautiful young man."

—JAVIER ZAMORA, author of *Solito*

"Exquisite, heartbreaking, incredibly beautiful . . . The whole narrative thrums with a bright, warm longing. You can feel the sunshine of LA and Iran, the rhythm of Khashayar J. Khabushani's voice. This is a novel to return to again and again."

—CALEB AZUMAH NELSON, author of *Open Water*

"A work of meticulous care and genuine candor, one that shies away from no earthly event, yet spiritually soars . . . To read it is to experience the contradictions of the weighty and the exalted, to witness a self forged by both brutality and love. Khabushani is a poetic visionary, as generous as he is brave."

—HEIDI JULAVITS, author of *Directions to Myself*

"Khashayar J. Khabushani has taken a coming-of-age story and flooded it with light. This is a gorgeous and wrenching debut from a writer I'll be following for many years to come."
—CATHERINE LACEY, author of *Nobody Is Ever Missing*

"Deeply moving and courageous, *I Will Greet the Sun Again* explores the sense of loss and violence inherent in the immigrant experience. It is an intimate and unflinching story about the ways in which we hurt each other and how we all need love and acceptance to survive."
—SAHAR DELIJANI, author of *Children of the Jacaranda Tree*

"A tender, heartbreaking portrait of a sweet child living in a broken world . . . Khabushani is an incredibly talented writer."
—IMBOLO MBUE, author of *Behold the Dreamers*

"A heartbreaking, cinematic, and original story of gathering and becoming oneself. But it's also a story of unraveling: the characters grow up, apart, and together again; they constellate a whole from which each individual eventually pearls off, like a drop of rain from a cloud. *I Will Greet the Sun Again* glimmers with wisdom and beauty and pain, and Khabushani has pulled off what only the very gifted can do—he has written a book that feels as dark, as light, and as alive as youth itself."
—ARIA ABER, author of *Hard Damage*

I Will Greet the Sun Again

I Will Greet the Sun Again

A Novel

Khashayar J. Khabushani

HOGARTH
London/New York

2024 Hogarth Trade Paperback Edition

Published in the United States by Hogarth, an imprint of Random House, a division of Penguin Random House LLC, New York.

HOGARTH is a trademark of the Random House Group Limited, and the H colophon is a trademark of Penguin Random House LLC.

Originally published in hardcover in the United States by Hogarth, an imprint of Random House, a division of Penguin Random House LLC, in 2023.

Library of Congress Cataloging-in-Publication Data
Names: Khabushani, Khashayar J., author.
Title: I will greet the sun again: a novel / Khashayar J. Khabushani.
Description: First edition. | London; New York: Hogarth, [2023]
Identifiers: LCCN 2022041305 (print) | LCCN 2022041306 (ebook) |
ISBN 9780593243329 (trade paperback) | ISBN 9780593243312 (ebook)
Classification: LCC PS3611.H313 I95 2023 (print) |
LCC PS3611.H313 (ebook) | DDC 813/.6—dc23
LC record available at lccn.loc.gov/2022041305
LC ebook record available at lccn.loc.gov/2022041306

Printed in the United States of America on acid-free paper

randomhousebooks.com

1st Printing

To my dream team,
who made this dream possible—

Bill Clegg
David Ebershoff
Parisa Ebrahimi
Martin Pousson
Isabel Wall

"Everything depends on how relentlessly one forces
from this experience the last drop, sweet or bitter, it
can possibly give. This is the only real concern of
the artist, to recreate out of the disorder of life that
order which is art."

—JAMES BALDWIN, *Notes of a Native Son*

"به آفتاب سلامی دوباره خواهم داد
به جویبار که در من جاری بود
می آیم می آیم می آیم.. . . . . .
و آستانه پر از عشق می شود"

"I will greet the sun again,
the stream that once flowed in me . . .
I will come, I will come, I will come
and the entrance will be filled with love."

—FOROUGH FARROKHZAD, "I Will Greet the Sun Again"

I

Named After a King

climb down the bunk ladder and leave the small room me and my brothers share. The apartment is still and stuffy and Maman is asleep on the living room floor. I head out the door, careful to close it quietly behind me.

In the courtyard I run my fingertips along the yellow stucco wall. On my forearm I have this bright bumpy scrape from when Shawn tackled me against the building playing Smear the Queer. It's like a tattoo and reminds me how good it feels to become older, tougher.

Early morning is the only time I get to be out of the apartment on my own. The Valley's sky is white and empty. A leaf blower runs loud somewhere. I can't see the city from here, but I know one day I'll have more than just these stucco walls and patches of brown grass.

For once the laundry room isn't coughing out its weird smelly steam. I take the pebble-stone staircase to the second floor, clearing two steps at a time. Back inside through a chalky metal door, down a sticky hallway and then another, stamping over brown soda stains and cigarette burns in the carpet.

I knock on Johnny's door loud enough for him to hear, but quickly. I don't want to bother his mom, who's probably pouring a cup of coffee, halfway through her first cigarette. She barely cracks the door open. Still getting his beauty sleep,

Cynthia says, a quick stream of smoke passing through her lips.

I'll come back later, I tell her and hurry back to our apartment before Baba gets home.

Maman hasn't woken up yet. Her breathing is silent and her face shiny with sweat. A thin beige bedsheet pulled up to her chin, her chest gently rising, Maman looks beautiful as she sleeps.

Shawn's sitting on the floor in front of the triple bunk Baba built for us, crunchy boogers in the corners of his eyes. He blows the snot from his nose onto the sleeve of his shirt.

And you wonder why girls don't like you, Justin says, leaning over from the top bunk. Shawn laughs and I do, too.

Shawn asks, Doesn't Johnny's mom get tired of you running upstairs and knocking on their door at the crack of dawn?

Like I haven't already thought of that myself. I don't want Shawn to come with me when I go back, so I lie and say, Nobody answered.

Shawn passes a controller up to Justin, whose scrawny legs are dangling over the wooden ledge. Justin asks Shawn for the millionth time why, if he doesn't like playing basketball in real life, he would want to in a video game?

What are you talking about? says Shawn. I love basketball. I just don't get to do it.

Why not? I ask.

Why do you think. Look the fuck around.

It's Friday, our last weekend of summer break. In the living room I hear Maman starting her morning. First folding up her bed, which isn't actually a bed, just a couple of sheets and a pillow on the floor and the thick fuzzy blanket she brought with her from Isfahan, then storing it all in the closet. She is setting the kettle on the stove for chai when Baba gets home.

Baba calls for me and my brothers, his voice booming through our bedroom walls.

I find Baba emptying out his pockets onto the floor. Dozens of twenty-dollar bills. More money than I've ever seen Baba have. His face is proud after a rare good night at the casino. We're going to celebrate, he promises. He walks over to the sofa, where we're not allowed to make a sound while he sleeps, slowly peeling off his crinkled button-up shirt and gray dress pants.

Maman stays seated at the dining table, eating her breakfast, the same one she has every morning. Noon barbari with paneer and walnuts and honey, always a plate of fresh sabzi on the side. A clip at the back of her head holds her long black curly hair. No makeup on and still Maman looks so pretty.

Are you hungry? she asks me, holding out a bite of bread covered with crumbly cheese.

A pot of tea sits on the samovar on the stove. She waits for it to finish steeping as I pick up a few of the twenty-dollar bills. When Baba isn't looking I hand one to Maman. She tucks it into her purse and brings a finger to her lips. We agree without words that we won't give the money back even if Baba asks.

Baba is now lying stretched out on the sofa with the back of his wrist over his forehead. I lean down to hug him, the smell of cigarette smoke heavy all around. He brings me close to his stubbly face and kisses me once on the cheek. His eyes are heavy and red with puffy bags. It looks like he's never going to wake once he falls asleep. I make sure to be quiet as I go to tell my brothers about all the money.

Instead of pausing the video game while I was gone, Shawn kept on playing.

You snooze you lose, he says.

He wasn't *snoozing*, you idiot, Justin says, still in bed. He was with Baba. What did he want? he asks me.

Baba hit the freaking jackpot, I say.

Yeah? Shawn says. How much you wanna bet by tomorrow morning the money's gone?

I tell Shawn he's wrong and so does Justin, pulling a crumpled bill from his Nowruz stash, which he keeps tucked underneath his mattress. He dangles it down at us. Five bucks says Baba keeps winning, he bets Shawn, who stands up from his bed. *Deal*. But don't go crying to him when I take your dough. Shawn spits into his palm and my brothers shake on it. I climb up into my bed to hide the money I kept for myself from Baba's jackpot. Johnny will be so impressed when I show him.

Baba marches into our room, clapping his hands. His shoulders are loose and his cheeks shiny from a fresh shave, the tiny bit of hair left on the top of his head combed to the side. He's wearing his gray slacks and a clean dress shirt, tucked deep into his waist. Tavalod, tavalod, tavalod-et mobarak, Baba chants, shutting off our game and swaying his body, dancing how he does at mehmoonis after the shirini has been served, the music turned up high. A Persian Happy Birthday just for me.

It's a week after my actual birthday, but Baba announces we're going to celebrate today just as he promised. Together, he says, like families are meant to.

I race down from my bunk, careful to skip the missing third step of the ladder. After seeing the *fuck you* Justin had carved into its wood, Baba hammered off the step. He didn't bother asking which one of us it was, then had the three of us line up together, facing our bunk, a shoe in his hand, and Justin didn't say a single word, just stood there taking it. I was crying the hardest even though Shawn got it the worst. As the oldest, Baba said, he's supposed to know better. Even though he's the oldest, Shawn is the shortest, shorter than Justin, even shorter than me.

Now standing beside him, I ask Baba to do his special Persian snap for me. Injoori, he shows me, bringing his thick and worn hands together. I watch and try to learn how he does it, the tip of his middle finger sliding against his index, where snaps like tiny firecrackers echo through our bedroom as he whistles. And now with Baba making music I lift my arms in the air, gently twisting and twirling my wrists, swaying my hips the way I've seen him do when he's taken his place in the middle of the dance floor, Baba always the first to bring life to the party.

How old? he asks, like he doesn't already know. I hold up a five and a four, showing him that I'm getting closer to Justin's ten and to Shawn's twelve. Any day now, Baba says, you'll become a man.

Mashallah, he chants, smiling even bigger, the top of his gums shiny and pink. His eyes are small as he dances, my body following his.

Maryam-jan, he yells, calling for Maman. Hurry and look, he says, come see your son.

Right here in our own building, Baba tells us, a grill and two benches, just for us. Doesn't—

Get any better than this, Shawn interrupts, finishing off Baba's favorite line. He walks out of our room, and Baba, Justin and me follow behind.

Maman joins us outside in our building's small picnic area. She has everything prepared. Sliced onions and tomatoes. Raw chicken shining bright gold with turmeric and oil. She wears her long black blouse and a scarf tied loosely around her hair. She fans the charcoal with a piece of cardboard, trying to get the coals to come to life. She asks Shawn to pick up the trash our neighbors left on the ground around us, which he does. Paper plates with spots of ketchup and used napkins, from whoever was here before.

For you, Baba says, handing me my birthday present as my brothers look on. A golden paper crown from Burger King. Baba knows it's my favorite.

He tells me to stand in front of the grill, says he wants a picture for Iran, for them to see just how handsome his youngest boy is.

Shawn sits on the old splintery bench to watch, telling me how stupid I look as Baba tells me where to place my arms.

Justin's already wandered off collecting dandelions that grow along the concrete path winding through our building. He likes bringing the ones that haven't yet died into our room, placing them by the window in the vase Maman let him have. Something nice to look at, he says. Our version of a hotel room.

Baba continues snapping, then scrolling the wheel on his camera, taking more pictures. When he finishes, he sets the camera aside and tells me to come to him. He grabs my shoulders and squeezes the muscles in my arms. Your brother's becoming so strong, he tells Shawn, then Baba leans in close, his bushy mustache tickling my cheek as he whispers into my ear, a secret only for us to know, that I'm his favorite. He says my name loud and long, as if he wants everyone in the building to hear. His youngest son, named after a Persian king, our very first and the very best, though I haven't felt any of that, not powerful or important the way a king is supposed to feel. Instead, each time Baba says my name it makes me want to disappear, so embarrassed, wanting to turn my back to whoever can hear. I hate the way my name sounds so foreign and old.

Which is why nobody but Baba uses my real name, not me, not Johnny or Christian, and not even the adults at school who stutter whenever they see it on the roll sheet. I tell them all to call me K, because unlike Baba and Maman I was born right here and like my brothers I want to be known as a boy from L.A., since that's the truth. Like Christian and Johnny, like my friends at school. And eventually I'll even have tattoos of my own, I'll wear a Dodgers jersey and sunglasses everywhere I go, I'll drink every kind of beer.

I ask Shawn, even though I already know the answer, why him and Justin got American names, and not me.

While you were in Maman's belly, Shawn says, grinning, Baba had this dream that you'd grow up to be Iran's next shah.

My brother thinks it's hilarious.

Baba checks on the onions and tomatoes on the grill, turning them over, yelling for Justin to come back. Shawn stands behind our dad and makes faces and Justin tries not to laugh. Maman tells me I should go and invite our neighbors.

This entire time I've been watching from the corner of my eye, hoping Johnny doesn't come out to hang out on the steps like he usually does. He'd see how strict Baba is with us and how serious he dresses, as if in this very moment we're on our way to the mosque for namaz. Johnny would see how different me and my brothers are, even though we act the same. Maman wearing a headscarf, Baba talking in Farsi, seeming more like a grandfather than a dad. He acts proud of it, too, as if being almost twenty years older than Maman is something to show off.

They aren't home, I tell Maman.

One by one Baba removes the pieces of barbecued chicken from the grill. He places them over the long sheet of sesame flatbread, letting the noon sangak absorb the juice dripping from the boneless chicken thighs.

What about the friends you're always going out to play with? Maman continues.

You mean Christian? Shawn asks.

Baleh. Maman nods. But the other one, too.

That's Johnny, Shawn reminds her.

Ask them—

Velesh kon, Baba says, interrupting. We don't have time, he tells Maman.

Baba tells us to follow him to the parking lot, says we can finish eating in the car. With plastic plates in our hands we begin to leave, but that's when I see him, sitting on the staircase. Johnny's wearing his fitted Dodgers cap, brim pulled low down to his eyebrows. His legs are open and wide, his arms resting at their elbows on his knees, palms down as if they're too big for his wrists to carry. He nods my way, the tiniest smile on his mouth.

If it were nighttime, his mom gone to work, he'd have a stolen Marlboro and would be taking long drags while watching the blue-black sky that gives us a few scattered stars if we're lucky. But for now Johnny sits there staring into nothing, copying the way we've seen the gangbangers in our neighborhood sitting on the curb outside of Lanark Park. Spines curved, bodies hunched forward with their heads slowly swiveling left to right, looking. Johnny does the same. Waits for the Valley's still and hot summer day to give him something, anything.

We drive through Malibu's canyon and into a short tunnel, where Baba punches down on the horn and glances over his shoulder at me and my brothers. A quick smile on his lips and our ritual begins, Baba telling us to let it all out, to make as much noise as we can.

But this time, instead of shouting I lower my window, feeling the cool darkness as we reach the end of the tunnel, the final echoes bouncing off my cheeks and jaw, and that's when Justin leans over, yelling at me to roll up the window because the drumming from the wind is hurting his head.

I don't listen to him. I keep going, looking up at the slivers of sunlight pouring through the tall green trees, until finally my brother reaches over, rolls up the window himself, and now my neck is stuck between the window frame and the glass, both of us laughing as I beg for mercy.

A few miles down Pacific Coast Highway Baba finds our spot, parks the car right here on the shoulder of the cliff. He puts the red metal lock in place on the steering wheel and hurries around to the trunk, takes out the Coleman camping stove to fire up for chai when we're down by the water. The three of us strip off our jeans, changing into shorts. I peek over at Shawn, wanting to know what it'll look like when I'm older, wondering if his has the same pink and brown as mine.

Baba is standing at the edge of the cliff. I join him and my brothers do, too, all of us lined up together in a row, and for a second I close my eyes, just listening. The water crashing onto shore, the ocean's big salty breath huffing through the wind. With my eyes closed the waves feel closer than they really are, as if the ocean's hum lives inside me, too. Until Shawn pretends to shove me off the cliff, scaring me good. Then Baba shows us three quarters in his open palm. Smiling so big he says, Whoever gets there first gets these.

Racing down the cliff's narrow dirt path, Justin is in the lead, though not by much. He's followed by Shawn and right behind there's me, skipping and jumping through the thick vines and dusty rocks, my naked feet landing with theirs. When we reach the beach Justin and me wrestle Shawn to the ground, scooping handfuls of sand and forcing them between his teeth while two women stare and ask, Don't these kids have parents?

Now I'm in the lead. Leaping over sandcastles and abandoned towels, arriving at the lip of the ocean. Justin follows and together we look back, waiting for Shawn. The sun throws its light onto our chests, heating our skin. Shawn finally arrives, his eyes red from the sand. Justin counts down from five, and I pinch my nostrils as we plunge into the waves, roaring—

It's so fucking cold, Shawn goes. And then Justin yells, I'm getting out.

Splashing them both I tread farther into the sea because once you go under, it isn't so bad. Floating near the shore, I watch my brothers. Justin walking along the water as Shawn collapses onto the sand, his body open and free, here for the sun.

And there's Baba, stumbling down the path from the top of the cliff. He drops the cooler off with Shawn and right away my brother pulls out a cola, snapping it open, holding up the can as its dark liquid rushes into his mouth and across his chin. He waits for it to rise from his gut, a burp so long and loud that the lifeguard sitting up high at her station will notice him. This is Shawn's favorite part of coming to the beach, winking at the girl of his dreams, the lifeguard shaking her blond head, laughing.

It doesn't get any better than this, Baba roars, driving his arms into the ocean, his knees kicking up high as he stomps his feet, setting off fireworks of salty mist that spray me, the white ocean birds hovering above. He scoops up handfuls of the sharp blue water, dumping them onto himself as if the water were God's, put here for prayer. Like this, Baba becomes clean again.

This time, he shouts, turning toward me—this time we're going all the way.

He wraps his arm around my shoulder as I join him, bringing my chilled skin into his. All the way out there, he tells me, pointing past the surfers drifting and waiting for the perfect wave, past the orange cone bobbing in the water and the lifeguard's red-and-white boat dashing across. My eyes follow his to the edge of the ocean, the shadowy blue water leaning up into puffed white clouds, long milky threads sketched across the bottom of the sky. Waves dipping and then folding into Baba's chest, he lowers himself into the ocean. A smile splashed across his face, I keep watching as he chants it again and again. It's perfect out here, Baba says, perfect.

He then points higher into the sky, the sun spreading its light through the clouds so bright, as Baba reminds me, again, how he saw it in my eyes from the very beginning, holding me in his arms after I was born, a light inside of me as strong as the sun.

He helps me climb onto his back, my arms wrapped and locked across his chest. I let my legs dangle and hang on as he stumbles to his feet, tightening his grip around my ankles, telling me that he's here, he's holding on.

Taking two steps back then shuffling his legs forward, Baba drives his toes deep into the sand, digs in his balance and I can feel each step crunching through his legs, snapping through his chest until they no longer do because now, we're floating. The ocean borrows our weight and carries us toward the end, the sting from the salt and the sun burning my eyes open.

Baba turns his neck, tells me to get ready. After that one gets here, he says, his eyes now focused on the wave coming toward us, follow me underneath.

But I thought you said we were going all the way, I tell him, my voice carried away by the wind—

Almost, he shouts. *Almost.*

My shoulders lean back, my body no longer huddled into Baba's. The bones in my chest stretching as I take bigger and longer bites of air, storing them inside while Baba drinks down his final breath, escaping below.

And so now I rise in the ocean's lap, higher and then higher as the wave curls and drapes over, tucking me inside what's now become a hushed blue cave. Where the ocean is quieter than Baba or my brothers will ever know.

Its blue skin becoming my own, the wave's white vein ripping through, and I watch as the cave begins to crack and then snap, spitting me out and thrashing my body, my face slamming onto the ocean floor and still—here underneath with this fire in my lungs, salt churning in my stomach, the ocean saying I told you so, told you so, you should have never come out this far—I don't close my eyes, don't ask for it to stop, I just keep watching. Waiting for it to happen again, that pretty moment where I was tucked inside of my own quiet, noticed.

Justin does it first, stripping off his pillowcase and telling us to do the same, says he has an idea for how to fall asleep. We've been tossing around in our bunks for what feels like forever, sweating. Our room's stuffy with heat, nothing's been working, no matter how close we bring the fan to our bed.

The later it gets the more awake I become, already feeling the burn in my eyes from when the alarm goes off early in the morning.

Me and Shawn do what our brother says, anything to make the heat go away. We leave our beds, stepping into the kitchen where we stand at the sink. Justin opens the freezer, dips his pillowcase underneath the running faucet, then stashes it inside.

Greatest shit you've ever thought of, Shawn says after a few minutes, sighing as he buries his face into Justin's pillowcase, then does the same with his and mine. He soaks them, puts them in the freezer, this time waiting even longer so that our pillowcases get even colder.

It's all gross now, I tell Justin, once we're back in our beds, the edges of my sheet quickly becoming damp.

And then, after a few more minutes of trying, I tell my brothers I can't sleep like this.

Here then, Shawn says, flinging up a tattered book from his bed. It's called *Slam!*

Since when do you read? Justin asks him.

I don't, our brother answers and I can hear in his voice how it's something he's proud of. Just this one and maybe you'll like it, too, he tells me, poking his toes into my mattress from underneath.

I hold the book up in front of me, using the streetlight that's coming through our window to see the words on the page. I turn to a random chapter of the book, somewhere in the middle, because whenever I read this is how I do it—I've never started from the beginning and finished a book all the way.

You got to be better than good, and you got to be hungry all the time. If you thinking about anything else than getting the ball and winning the game, it says, *you gone.*

I keep reading, reading about a place that sounds like ours, kids hanging out on cracked steps, the way we do with Johnny and Christian, and it makes sense why Shawn keeps this book with him, tucked under his mattress, reading about basketball after he's finished playing.

And the more of the chapter I read the more it feels like this is a book I might actually finish. The boy telling the story is seventeen and six foot four and he goes by the name Slam, has the kind of voice where it feels like what he's saying isn't fake, or exaggerated the way Christian likes to talk. I don't know why, or how, but I can tell the difference. So I turn back to start from the very first page, no longer caring whether I fall asleep for our first day of school, staying up with Slam's voice instead.

. . .

When the alarm goes off it's still the part of the morning that's dark, cold after the night was so hot, my bed too comfortable to leave. I stay right here, my blanket pulled to my chin, listening as Justin climbs down from his bunk. He switches on the light, the sudden brightness hurting my eyes. He's the first to get dressed and Shawn isn't even awake yet.

Justin tucks his white collared shirt into his dark blue Dickies, buckles his belt to keep the waist of his pants high above his belly button, the way Baba taught us. I lift my chin and rest it on the wooden railing of my bed. Can you turn off the light? I ask. Justin looks up, a quiet smile on his face. Hello to you, too, he says.

Baba comes in to check on us, to make sure that last night we set aside our backpacks, with our clothes stacked there in the corner by the door, folded and neat, ready. Zoodbash, he says, telling us to hurry.

He goes back into the living room with Justin to finish making chai, already the smell of warm sugar and cardamom fills our apartment. I climb down from my bunk without bothering to hold on to the sides of the ladder and I should've known better because as I reach my foot past the missing third step it doesn't land where I expect, causing me to lose my balance and fall. The side of my head lands straight on the floor, crumbs and dust from our carpet sticking to my face. What's so funny, I say to Shawn who's now laughing in his bed, the kind of laugh where for twenty seconds straight he can't catch his breath but finally when he does, he shakes his head and says, Look at you, his laugh still going as he peels his boxers off and reaches for the towel he keeps hanging from the ladder.

Baba is back, checking on us again. One more minute, he announces.

So much for looking fresh for my first day, Shawn mutters, putting his boxers back on.

Shawn keeps a plastic basketball hoop hanging from the closet door. I open it and put on the clothes he wore last year. His white polo with scattered stains impossible to wash off, cargo shorts that I wear even when it's cold, like it is this morning.

In the kitchen there's a glass of tea for each of us, and Baba's keeping his voice low because Maman is still asleep, he says she only got home an hour ago. She's been working at the hospital as a nurse's assistant and in the afternoons, before her shifts, she's been taking classes that she says will further her license. I flip through her textbook on top of the kitchen counter, pictures of the human body and long descriptions of its details, and I can hardly understand any of it. Maman's English isn't anywhere near as good as ours and she's still passing in school.

I ask Baba if he's found a job yet, if that's why he has to take us to school so early, but he shakes his head. I don't get why, though—why if Baba's the best engineer in all of America, like he says he is, Boeing would let him go. It's been almost two years and he still hasn't found a new job. Don't worry so much, Baba tells me when I ask if we'll ever get to move back to our house. Baba's going to take care of everything, he says.

· · ·

19

I'm the first to line up outside our classroom's slanted bungalow. Our teacher hasn't arrived yet and the morning's still gray and dark. I wait for the sun to break out. Even when the sky is cloudy and wet it eventually does, and sometimes there's a faded rainbow, both ends quietly disappearing behind the mountains.

Standing alone with my teeth chattering in the cold, I hate that I have to be here at school while Maman is at home, warm inside our apartment. By now she's probably up setting the table for breakfast, the smell of hot bread in the oven. Drinking chai and watching the morning dew dribbling down the living room's windows. I wish I could be at home with her, my brothers and Baba not around to bother us, helping Maman do the chores before she goes to work, her telling me how helpful I am, how happy she is that I'm her son.

The rest of the class slowly starts to show up. They stand in line behind me, showing off their new sneakers and trading stories from summer. I stay facing toward the bungalow, hiding the stains on my polo. I won't let them see the front of my body until it's tucked behind my desk. I learned from last year, it's impossible to make friends or keep crushes if on the first day your new classmates see that your clothes are dirty.

Now our teacher walks up the small metal ramp, getting our attention as the ramp wobbles loud and clacks beneath her heels. She waits for us to form a perfect straight line before opening the classroom door, all of us marching in behind Ms. Kim.

Inside, where taped across the wide back wall of our classroom there are posters of what we'll be studying, the Oregon Trail and the Gold Rush, a poster of MLK giving his I Have a Dream speech and one with a man in a tall hat pointing, saying he wants us for the U.S. Army, the cozy hush of a new school year warms up my arms and legs.

We find the seats we've been assigned to, each with a colorful plastic pencil box that has our name on it. Ms. Kim talks to us in a way that makes it feel like she's known us all along. She's already memorized who we are, already knows to call me K before I have to ask.

She says she expects us to put our best foot forward, doesn't matter how the other fourth-grade classes are spending their first day. We'll begin with a spelling bee, she tells us, to see who kept up with their summer reading.

What reading? I whisper to the boy with the short spiky hair sitting to my right. His clothes smell like the playground's black pavement.

He shrugs his shoulders. I guess we're screwed, he tells me.

Ms. Kim takes her place in front of the chalkboard, carefully wiping the smudges of chalk from her black blouse. She doesn't say a single word, allows the buzz of chatter sweeping through our classroom to continue, and only when the chatter comes to a complete stop does she begin.

The winner, Ms. Kim explains, keeping her voice low, will receive a prize of twenty raffle tickets. Which, she tells us, walking toward the back of the room with each of us following her every step, can be used for the gift shop.

She opens one of the closets to reveal the things she's purchased for us. Shelves stocked from top to bottom, new glittery pencils, fresh eraser caps and scratch-and-sniff stickers, rulers and scissors and stacks of fancy construction paper.

Open during lunch and recess, Ms. Kim says, removing a few of the prizes to show us their marked prices.

My eyes reach the top shelf, where there's a navy blue T-shirt hanging on display. It has our school's logo on it, which means that it meets dress code even though it doesn't have a collar. I add up how many spelling bees I'll have to win to buy the shirt. That way I'll no longer have to wear Shawn's from last year, which was a size too big for him even then. Well, Ms. Kim says, closing the door to the shop. Shall we begin?

She still hasn't gotten to the bigger words on her list, but already most of the class is out, a few didn't even bother trying to spell the word they were given. When it got to their turn they just sat there staring back at Ms. Kim as she waited, until eventually they dropped their heads down into their folded arms, keeping them there on the desk.

Which is why I'm able to make it to the very end, where it's just me and one other girl, Crystal, who's sitting in the first row. And though Ms. Kim doesn't say it, you can tell she's disappointed in our class.

Captain, Ms. Kim announces.

Crystal spells it out, doesn't even wait for Ms. Kim to use the word in a sentence.

She gets the nod from our teacher and there's a roar of applause, Crystal's friends cheering her on.

The attention comes straight back to me. My legs won't stop rattling, and my hands feel freezing cold. But even though I'm nervous I love how the attention of the whole class is on me and Crystal, love how they're staring and whispering, making bets on who's going to win.

Across, Ms. Kim says.

That morning, they drove across the Golden Gate Bridge.

So easy, I think to myself, and I can hear the boy next to me whispering the same. Saying that I got lucky, it isn't fair.

My voice catching, excited to get closer to my navy blue shirt, I can already feel the freshness of its fabric, the way it'll smell new on my skin. I start to spell out my word but then pause, realize that I'm being tricked, I remember how there are two *C*'s in *accross*, not just one.

So I start over and spell it out with two *C*'s this time, and I wait for the applause, for our teacher to give Crystal her next word, but instead she announces Crystal the winner, our class's spelling bee champion.

There's been a mistake, I'm about to say as Ms. Kim scribbles my word on the board, spelled the correct way.

Crystal stands from her chair and walks toward my row, coming up to my seat. Her white polo, like mine, is also too big for her, loose on her body with its short sleeves reaching past her elbows. There's a small scar above her left eyelid. I want to ask her what happened.

I knew you'd be the one who'd make it to the final round with me, she says, tucking bits of her long and shiny black hair behind her ears.

She holds out her hand, smiling with her lips together, one small dimple beginning to form, but she isn't showing off the way I expected her to, isn't telling the rest of the class I'm dumb for missing such an easy word. Instead, as I shake her hand she's telling me how much fun it was. Now her small square teeth are showing, bright, and I never knew I was shy but here I am blushing in front of her, my head tilted down.

You, too, I mutter, knowing I'm not making any sense, and that makes me blush even more.

Ms. Kim is up in front of the board, holding two fingers in the air to get our attention. I scribble what Crystal said onto the surface of my desk, so I don't forget. To tell Baba, later today when he comes to pick me up from school, that even before I made it to the very last round, the spelling bee champion in our class already knew that I would.

At first, Christian told me, it starts in your pits.

So I stand in front of the sink to check, stretching my arm up and behind my neck, leaning over and getting as close to the mirror as I can. It should have hit by now, he said, and not only should I have armpit hair, but my balls should have dropped, too. So I lied and said that they have.

Luckily I have proof, tucked in the very center of my armpit, the tiny hairs starting to sprout, a small shadow of my new manhood. I run my fingers over them, admiring puberty more and more until I notice that it gets lost, erased.

Because it isn't hair, I finally realize, just all that dirt from the hours this morning playing on the blacktop with Shawn, sweating.

So I check for my Adam's apple, maybe I just haven't noticed it yet. In my throat does anything vibrate when I talk?

When I asked Johnny if I could feel his—he's older than me by three years, so he would know—I could feel his Adam's apple vibrating, round and pointed, perfect.

Looking out the bathroom door and making sure Justin and Shawn are still asleep, that way they don't ask me why I'm taking so long, I pull down my shorts, checking to see if my pubes are here.

Nothing, still bare, smooth. But it shouldn't be, Christian said. There should be pubes, lots of them.

I cup my nuts, both fitting snug into the center of my palm. I don't think my balls have dropped, not yet.

Putting down its cover and sitting on the toilet, my boxers lowered down to my ankles, I want to try it.

I can't find lotion, so I use soap instead.

Feels even better with spit, Christian said, but I don't want it to be so dirty.

I tear off a sheet of toilet paper and keep it ready by my side. You'll need it for after, Christian warned me. For when it gets all over your tummy, he said, laughing.

I rub my hands with the soap, making them warm, making sure the head of my penis is between my palms because the rim is where it feels best. I slide my palms back and forth, fast and hard, this is how you make yourself feel good, how you get yourself to finish, Christian told me.

I close my eyes, easier that way to imagine a body rubbing against where I'm hard, and it surprises me that Johnny's is the one that comes to mind.

The pressure growing inside, building and building and I can't stop smiling, can't believe it's happening.

Rising from the bottom of my penis, my first load of cum moving up to the very tip, but Christian didn't say I would have to push or that it would pinch and that the tip would burn, but maybe he left that part out on purpose, Christian would do something like that.

So I squeeze and push and ignore the burn until it spills all over my lap and onto my stomach, splashing into my face and leaking down from my chin to my shorts, the warm and sour piss I was holding in all along.

t's Friday and we're free, finished with school for the week. Shawn is lying on the sofa, practicing his form, using his right hand to shoot his Spalding into the air, flicking his wrist and following through, back and forth, back and forth. I time it perfectly, snatch the ball before it lands in his hand, dribbling through the living room and using a spin move to keep the ball protected when he gets up from the sofa and tries to steal it back.

He's chasing me down the hallway, where he slips and falls, banging his chin against the floor.

You just got your ankles broken. I laugh at Shawn, pointing down and he's grinning too because he knows I got him good.

Baba shouts from the bathroom, where he's cutting Justin's hair, telling me to get ready for my turn because he's almost done.

Soon the sun is going to set and I know we need to hurry, if not we'll miss Maghrib prayer, but Shawn and me are feeling too good to listen to Baba.

Justin walks out from the bathroom, his hairline crooked, some parts of his head darker than others, spots that were missed. He tries his best to hide how he's about to start crying, the spiky hair he spent all summer growing out now gone.

There are clumps of his black hair still scattered on the chair when I take my seat. The clipper's teeth get stuck as soon as Baba begins, but he pushes it through and it feels like a fire crawling through my scalp as my hair gets pulled, as my head jerks back. My eyes start to fill, I grind my jaw and swallow down the tears that are trying to come up, making sure not to move. Baba doesn't like it when we squirm or wiggle in the chair, doesn't like it when we cry or wince.

Your turn, I tell Shawn who's waiting outside the bathroom. After Baba's finished with all three haircuts we throw away the newspapers scattered on the floor, we clean and sweep until no hair is left. We take turns rinsing off, putting on the same polo shirts we wear to school, tucked in.

As always, Maman stays behind when we leave for the mosque, says it's better for her to pray at home.

On Topanga, we walk past the Pic 'n' Save, then the KFC, Justin pausing for a quick moment to wave at the couple we met on Monday when he and I walked home from school. An elderly woman and man, their skin cracked and red, by the same plastic bench at the same bus stop where they take turns sleeping, a cart and black garbage bags beside them.

Without them having to ask, Justin gave the couple the leftover change he had in his pockets and it made me feel bad, not having anything to give. I had spent my two quarters at recess on a chocolate chip cookie, splitting it with Crystal.

Baba pauses at the gate in front of the mosque, holding out his arm to stop us from walking in. Without school, he says, pointing at the couple, using them as a chance to give us a lesson, that will be your life.

·   ·   ·

We follow Baba into the area in the back that's reserved for wudu, a big bathroom with faucets lined along the wall. I watch as he splashes his face and rubs water between his toes, and I do the same, making sure to get clean for God as the imam's call for Maghrib prayer comes echoing through.

Baba hands us each a prayer stone from the straw basket by the door, what he calls mohr, a stone that he says is made of the earth's soil. I hold it in my palm, running my fingers over the Arabic that's engraved on its surface. The stone is soft to the touch, cool against my skin. I place it at the front of the rug, there to guide me, for when we kneel and place our foreheads onto the floor, reminding ourselves about the Day of Judgment, of God's compassion and wisdom.

As we line up beside Baba, he nudges Justin and Shawn closer to the line marked in the soft green carpet. I tell myself not to look because I already know Shawn's making faces, trying to make us laugh, so I bite the insides of my cheeks, making sure I don't crack. My brother hates standing here, the prayer room stuffy with men. Shawn says they stink, especially when their bottoms are sticking in our faces during prayer, which is why both he and Justin scoot farther and farther back.

But me, I like being this close, the smell of damp beards and freshly washed skin, so close that when the men bend over, placing their hands on their knees before kneeling to the floor, I'm the only one who gets to look, since everyone else, Baba included, is focusing on God.

The game already started, and now Shawn's pissed that he's missing it. Our small black TV is blaring on full volume. That way he can at least listen to the announcer, hear what's happening as the Lakers win the tip-off.

It wasn't Justin's fault, I tell Shawn as he presses a piece of gauze against my right eyebrow, soaking up the blood, I'm the one who used his stuff without asking.

Doesn't mean he had to slam that shit into your face, Shawn says. And in my head I see it happening again, that look on Justin's face when he snatched his CD player from my hands, hitting me in the eye with it as if I was a thief.

I got lucky that Shawn was in his bed when it happened, 'cause right away he leapt up and shoved Justin off our bunk's ladder, telling him to get out of the room. And when Justin didn't listen, staring up at me instead, Shawn pushed him again, only this time making sure to keep his voice low. That way Baba didn't hear, didn't find out we were fighting, because if he did, it'd only make things worse. So instead it was Shawn who went to the cabinet in the bathroom, where Maman keeps her nursing supplies, grabbing the things he needed to get the bleeding to stop.

Before putting on a Band-Aid, Shawn narrows his mouth and blows onto my face, the soft, cool air making it feel so much better.

When Baba calls out for us, saying Maman needs our help in the parking lot to unload groceries, Shawn coaches me, Tell him you got elbowed while we were playing one-on-one—cool?

I nod, and my brother says not to worry, promising me that the cut won't leave a mark.

But even if it does, he says, slapping me on the shoulder, now with a smirk on his face as he stands to throw out the bloodied wads of cotton, it won't make you any uglier than you already are. He cracks up, making me smile, too.

Justin's already out in the parking lot with Maman. The closer Shawn and me and Baba get the bigger she smiles. Still in her light blue nurse's uniform, she's leaning against the trunk of our car, and on the pavement there aren't bags of groceries but three brand-new bikes, standing on their kick-stands. Their orange paint gleaming in the sunlight, the shine from the tire rims so bright I can't even look at them straight.

Now they can't complain that we don't buy them nice things, Maman tells Baba, smiling and running the back of her hand over my cheek. I got a big discount when I applied for their credit card, Maman adds, knowing Baba is always searching for a good bargain.

Turning to Justin—who's now smiling even though a few moments earlier he wanted to beat my ass—Shawn tells him, Go get Johnny and Christian. And make sure they bring their bikes, too, he shouts as Justin sprints into our building.

Baba grabs hold of one of the Huffys, inspecting its frame and the tires, pulling on its chain. Baba can tell if a bike is well made, worth the money or if it's just a piece of junk.

What credit card are you talking about? he asks Maman.

The Kmart in Northridge, she says. She shows Baba the receipt she pulls from her purse, crumbled and torn.

It was a huge promotion, she says as she smiles, twenty-five percent off. Can you believe that?

I run my fingertips over the metal handlebars, waiting for Maman to say she only rented them. That these bikes aren't ours and we'll have to return them.

But she doesn't. Just keeps humming along to her favorite Persian singer, Googoosh's voice spilling from the speakers of our white and rusted Corolla.

Boro digeh, she tells Shawn and me, shooing us away with her hand, loosening her headscarf and letting the breeze blow through her hair.

I leap onto my bike and Shawn does the same, the kickstand scraping against the concrete as I stumble to click it into its place.

My brother has a small head start but as we lap around the parking lot I pass him, using the speed bumps in the pavement as mini-ramps to jump from, going as high as I can. Riding past and yelling out for Maman to watch, I want her to see my body as it shoots up from my seat, my chin in the air, but with Baba standing so close to her face, she can't hear me.

Pedaling harder I slice through the warm soft wind, circling around the lot, faster and faster until the muscles in my legs scream, and just then Christian and Johnny join us on the black pavement with their bikes, Justin sprinting behind them and racing toward his.

It's about fucking time, Christian shouts. And now to show off I dare Johnny to catch me, standing even taller on my bike, I cruise with my face tilted toward the sky and I swear I can even feel the neighbors who live upstairs watching us from their windows, jealous, watching as Johnny gets closer from behind and I slow down so that he can.

When we circle back to the car, where Maman is still standing, the music is now gone, and I can hear Baba telling her she shouldn't have bought these bikes, that money is tight. Shawn was right when he said that Baba would lose the money he won at the casino.

Baba takes the keys and opens the trunk of our car, as Christian rides up, lifting the end of his wifebeater to wipe the sweat from his forehead. He looks at me and then my brothers, acting as if there's nothing happening. Let's dip, he tells us, talking over Baba who's continuing in Farsi, telling us to help him load up the trunk with our bikes.

As Christian nudges my shoulder he stares straight at Baba, not breaking eye contact. And I do the same, waiting. Baba holds my eyes with his and this time, finally, he's the one who pauses. Breaking into a forced smile he tells us to go, changing his mind about the bikes, at least for the moment.

Behind us, the black sliding gate of the parking lot inches open, one of our neighbors pulling into its entrance. Follow me, Johnny shouts, racing ahead.

We don't give Baba or even Maman a chance to tell us no, the three of us following Christian and Johnny, barely making it as I slip through on my bike, the last one out, just before the gate seals shut.

Baba yells for us but Justin says to keep riding. He's the one who told us to go, my brother says, grinning and standing up from his bike as the wind kisses his face.

Shawn shrugs his shoulders, It's true. He glances back

at Baba who's now walking toward our apartment, Maman watching from afar.

When we reach the end of our block on Gault Street, ready to turn back, Johnny says we gotta keep going, tells us there's somewhere he's always wanted to show us.

He leads the way onto Topanga, the farthest we've ever gone without our dad. We pass by the mosque, and then the KFC Baba took us to after prayer, where the three of us shared mashed potatoes and gravy, a biscuit for each of us. American boys, Baba called us as he watched us eat our dinner, handing us napkins while we licked our buttery fingers.

Out on our own, even the palm trees look different, taller, their long trunks swaying in the wind as if they're going to snap. And the metal electric tower we've driven past a million times . . . I never realized how big it is, the size of an entire block, with all these power lines stretching across Sherman Way.

We ride into the auto shop on the corner, waiting as Christian goes to the vending machine to buy a Sprite for us all to share, and I can tell this isn't his first time doing this because the men working don't even bother looking up, as if Christian's one of the employees.

The only place that would hire him without papers, Christian tells us, pointing to his uncle who's removing the bolts on a car's flat tire, the power drill's *zzzt-zzzt* that we're always hearing go off in our neighborhood. Maybe Christian's telling us about his uncle because he thinks Baba's the same, not able to get a job since he doesn't have papers. For our dad it's different, though. He could work anywhere, anytime he wants, he just chooses not to. Better to be your own boss, Baba's always saying.

We turn onto Bassett Street where the L.A. River cuts through, throwing down our bikes onto the dirt path, then crawling through a tiny space underneath the wiry gate. The five of us sit at the top of the concrete slope watching the water go by, which is less like a river and more like an outdoor sewer. But I don't say anything about the nasty smell, happy to be here with my brothers and our friends, next to this moving stream of slimy green water I didn't know the Valley had, seeing Canoga Park through Christian's and Johnny's eyes while above us a family of crows searches for their dinner.

Keep an eye on our bikes, Christian says to me and my brothers, nudging Johnny to stand up. We'll be right back, he tells us.

He and Johnny walk down the slope to the edge of the water, taking it to where there's a hidden spot underneath the short bridge, where I recognize the older guys from Canoga's gang in Raiders and Dodgers jerseys tagging up the walls of the Wash, the three of them with their girlfriends. Shawn tells me not to stare but I can't stop. Christian nods his head and takes a seat next to the one who looks the oldest, tattoos on his face and neck. Christian lowers his hoodie and shows off his fresh shaved head, cut all the way down to his scalp which shines with an ugly skin-green. He's only fourteen but the way he keeps his chest straight and stiff, accepting a swig of beer, it looks as though Christian's already an adult. And they're even more impressed with Johnny, who brought his own can of spray paint in his back pocket, tagging up the walls while one of the girlfriends shouts how cute he is. She then takes him into her arms, passing him a cigarette which he accepts, finishing it off.

I watch as they talk without saying much, the oldest one looking at Johnny, nodding, a quick handshake passing between them. At first I didn't believe him, when Johnny told me that he comes here at night, too, whenever his mom's boyfriend crashes at their apartment, though now I see that it's true. He isn't afraid of the Wash.

We stay out until the sun begins to go down even though we know Baba's going to be pissed, and that we'll probably have to pay for this, big time. Still, it's our first Sunday afternoon on our own, and with my brand-new Huffy gleaming on its kickstand next to me, I can feel myself becoming the American boy I want to be, just like Baba said we are.

When Johnny and Christian come back, I ask them how long it's been since they started hanging out with Canoga's gang, but Christian just laughs off my question, especially after I ask if next time he'll invite me down to hang out with them underneath the bridge.

ach time Baba tilts his head down, looking so broken, I turn to watch him. The way he's slumped in his chair, palms held out, as though he's trying to hand off his sadness.

It's not even noon and already the kitchen is baking from the sun. Maman reaches over to the window to lift the blinds, a warm breeze slipping through, the tea humming on the stove, the water in the samovar whistling up a thick steam.

Early this morning Baba got a call letting him know that last night at a hospital in New York an old classmate of his, David, passed away. David was Baba's closest friend from when he lived in New York City, he tells us, they were students together at Columbia. He and David lived on campus with each other for three whole years.

Now as my brothers and me sit here Baba lets us know how sorry he is for not going to New York when David asked him to. He runs his hand over his face, pinching at his eyes, asking Maman in a low voice to bring medicine for the headache he says won't go away.

After a long and loud gulp of water, Baba then sits up in his chair, straightening his shoulders. He looks at me, and then Justin and Shawn, as if in our silence he expects us to make him feel better, as if he's testing me and my brothers, waiting to see if one of us is going to crack and talk when the right thing for any of us to do is to stay quiet.

But for how much longer, I want to ask, will we have to sit here, switching between looking at one another and then down at our own hands, doing our best to keep from squirming in our seats.

I know that Justin wants to leave, too. He's been doing his best to hide the top of his head in the folds of his arms, so far he's gotten away with it. A month and a half since Baba's buzzed our heads, I wonder if he notices now how Justin's been spiking up his hair again, if he'll drag my brother by his ear to the bathroom and force him to wash it out. Baba says using gel makes us look zesht, trashy like the kids in our building whose families he tells us don't uphold any kind of standards. But I like the way it makes my brother look, his thin black hair so different from me and Shawn's, ours growing thick and puffing out, hard to style, hard to do anything with. I've told him, too, in the morning when he spikes up his hair before going to school, that it's hard to tell he's Iranian, which makes Justin smile big, he says that's the point.

Now I turn over to Shawn, and when I mouth to him that we should leave and go outside, he reminds me by widening his eyes and gritting his teeth to stop, to keep my mouth closed, quit rattling my legs underneath the table. He knows that if I break our quiet, asking Baba if we can be dismissed, all three of us will get disciplined. So I lower my head, trying my best to be a good brother for Justin and Shawn, to disappear into myself, wait for Baba to finish doing whatever it is he expects us to help him with by sitting here.

Javooni, Baba whispers and again opens out his palms.

Youth, he says, shaking his head slow, look away and then it slips right through your fingers.

He's staring straight into my eyes, like he wants me to say something, so I ask our dad why he didn't go to New York when he had the chance, all this year without work and he could have been there with David, could've taken us on our first trip outside of L.A.

The thin blue rings circling Baba's brown eyes glisten and glow, and I watch anger spreading over his face and cheeks. Then, to show us what happens when we ask him questions he doesn't want, he hits the table with his fist, causing one of its legs to beat into my knee. I jump, staring at where his tea has spilled, as wisps of steam weave away from the dark wood. Maman rushes to the kitchen for a rag, and Baba scoots his chair away from the table, standing up. I lower my head for what he's going to do to me, clenching my jaw.

But Shawn starts, too, breaking apart the quiet to get Baba's attention off me. We want to go with you one day, he tells our dad, causing Baba to pause. You've told us about New York but we've never gotten to see it for ourselves.

Now Baba takes the rag from Maman's hand, placing it in front of me, telling me to soak up the spilled tea from the table. Sitting back down, he breathes in deep and continues pouring out what's inside of him, me and my brothers silent again as Baba lays his anger on the table, as if it's something special for us to see.

t's just me and Shawn in the library after school, Justin left us to sit in a different section. He meant it when he said he wouldn't be helping me anymore, that from now on I'd have to study on my own. He's halfway through his project for the science fair and says he's got his eye on winning first place.

Baba thinks by making us come to the library instead of going straight home we'll work harder, become smarter, but sitting here after being in school all day I'm so bored, I tell Shawn, Let's go to where the computers are.

An older man one table over shushes me, setting down the magnifying glass he's using to read, pointing to the sign that says talking isn't allowed. My brother stuffs down his laughter, I whisper to c'mon but he shoos me away, opens his notebook and goes back to his writing.

I leave for the computers on my own, and after playing Tetris for a while—each time making it to level seven, when the blocks start dropping too fast for me to keep up—finally I look at the small digits on the corner of the screen and see that it's 7:30. I've been playing for an hour and a half straight and I still have Ms. Kim's math homework to do and haven't even started Baba's assignment that Justin and Shawn have probably finished by now.

Every night our dad makes us do five pages of writing,

copying down the sentences from a book we get to choose as long as it's by one of the writers he approves of, a list he still keeps with him years after taking his fancy classes at Columbia. Ibsen or Shakespeare or Wilde, the book always ends up being dusty and old, its pages cracked, yellow and smelly like dry scrambled eggs and marked up with highlighter and notes in the margins.

Ripping out five sheets from my spiral notebook, I hurry, scanning the spines of the books in the English section. I go to the librarian's desk and ask if I can borrow a pair of scissors.

I've seen Justin do this before, shortening the height of the paper by trimming off several lines to make the assignment shorter. Because what happens is by the middle of the first page my hand starts to hurt, my fingers cramping from trying to keep the pencil steady and perfectly in place. Baba says our writing has to be the very best, bold and clear and aligned within the margins, or else he won't accept it.

And what for? the librarian asks, blowing her nose into a crumbled white tissue while staring at me the whole time, raising her red-dyed eyebrows.

An assignment for my art class, I lie.

Pulling the scissors out from her drawer, Why don't you bring your assignment here, she says, and I'll help you cut whatever it is you need to cut.

When I don't say anything back the librarian displays the scissors for me. These are very sharp, she tells me, and I wouldn't want you to hurt yourself. Go on now. She smiles again.

Back at the table, I stare at my papers, worried she won't

believe me. I do it anyway, I go back to the librarian's desk and I hand her Baba's assignment, I tell her I need the bottom five lines cut from all five pages.

That's very peculiar, she says, still holding on to the scissors, gripping the long silver blades. I've never heard of a teacher asking for such a thing, she tells me, looking me up and down.

I glance at the clock on her desk, 7:39.

She looks over at Shawn, who's laughing at me and shaking his head.

It's too late. The librarian knows I'm lying and she won't give me the scissors, won't even cut the papers for me, asking now for me to go bring my guardian, as if I'm not running out of time. And when Baba comes to pick us up and sees that I rushed his assignment, my writing messy and forced, he'll tell us to get out of the car and stand facing the wall of the library building. And again as I do my best not to make a single sound, I'll remind myself that when I'm older I'll get to write how *I* want to write, stories that aren't old or long or in English that's hard to understand. I want to write using my own rules and not the way Baba says I'm supposed to, perfect and neat.

Justin said he would do it and he proved himself right. At school today he received first place in the annual science fair, and now on our walk home he holds up his ribbon the entire time, waving it in the sky as if it's a flag and he the leader of his country, declaring victory.

When we get to our apartment he doesn't even bother taking off his shoes, right away he goes to Maman who's sitting on the sofa, sewing the hole in one of Shawn's socks.

Holding the ribbon in her hands, for a moment she glances up with a flash of a smile, nodding her approval, taking off her glasses and setting down the thread and needle to give Justin a hug.

She tells him to place it on the Haft-sin for Baba to see, the table she set up for Nowruz, where my brother slides it between the tiny dishes of sumac and garlic and vinegar, checking on the bowl of lentils, all of us still waiting for the grass to sprout.

When Baba gets home and sees Justin's first-place ribbon, he comes into our room and tells us to meet him outside by the car. He says he has a surprise for us.

We drive to Reseda Boulevard where we stop at Burger King for a Whopper and a large order of fries. Baba cuts the burger into four equal parts, for me and my brothers to share, and right away Shawn decides it should be Justin who gets to

43

have the extra piece, since he's the reason we get to have this treat to begin with.

I finish first, and quickly, scarfing down my portion of the fries, staring over at Shawn's.

Mashallah, Baba says, placing his heavy hand on my knee, smiling at how big my appetite is.

I ask Baba if we can have one more burger, letting him know I'm still hungry. He shakes his head. If you don't learn to stop you'll make yourself fat, he tells me, now sliding his hand over my stomach as if he's checking to make sure I haven't gained weight. I regret even asking, the way Justin and Shawn are looking at me, laughing.

When my brothers finish, Baba smiles and tells us that we're going to Chuck E. Cheese, where we'll get to have the entire evening to ourselves.

And even though it's just a few days before Persian New Year, we know not to ask Baba for money, don't even bring it up. You don't need money to have fun, is what he always tells us.

After dropping us off out front, Baba cuts the car engine and tells us to wait. Reaching into his back pocket, he pulls out his brown leather wallet. Takes his time, making sure we're watching as he carefully unfolds the money he keeps tucked inside, his eyes on me and Shawn, telling us we have Justin to thank as he hands our brother a crisp new five-dollar bill.

No freakin' way, Shawn yells as the three of us sprint toward the entrance.

Inside, Justin cashes in his money while Shawn and I head straight for the ball pit. A secret of ours, we know if we search the bottom long enough eventually we'll find tokens that have been left behind. So we hold our breath, sinking below and scanning the floor for the abandoned coins that slipped from the pockets of the other kids who were jumping and diving into the ball pit before us and not noticing what they lost.

Our way of having fun for free, Shawn says when I show him what I found. A single token for us.

I sprint to the arcade to give the token to Justin. Out of the three of us, Justin is the best at getting the most tickets, he's able to zone in and focus. It's the same arcade game he plays each time, doesn't bother with the others and always he comes so close to hitting the jackpot.

The grand prize is at 387, the highest we've ever seen it, but he's already spent the money Baba had given him. I hand him one more chance, if Justin hits the button at the exact right moment, landing on the option marked *jackpot,* we'll each be able to get our own cotton candy.

He looks at me before sliding in the coin, Here it goes, and I watch from over his shoulder. Shawn joins us, too, and we huddle around our brother, his palm hovered over the glowing button, keeping his eyes on the bright purple light that circles around and around the lit board. Like this he waits, patient, his tongue curled over the top of his thin lip, waiting for the exact right moment. And even though the light is catching more speed, Justin doesn't seem nervous. He keeps his hand still and his eyes frozen. There's no rush, he whispers to himself.

Only now it's too late because the light is going way too fast, impossible for him to catch it on the jackpot. We're going to end up with one of the lower numbers, ten, twenty or thirty tickets to share between us, if we're lucky. I turn away, trying my best to ignore the kids in the arcade who are walking around holding plastic cups brimming with gold coins, tomato sauce smudged on their cheeks after scarfing down hot cheese pizza.

My eyes begin to fill, I can practically taste the cotton candy on my tongue, only now knowing there won't be much to show for the token I found, nothing for us to do as we wait for Baba to pick us up—

Sharp and sudden, first it's the sound of the alarm, ringing throughout the arcade, announcing *jackpot*. And then tickets that keep spilling and spilling from the machine's black slot. The two boys playing air hockey next to me abandon their game and so does the girl with red hair who's pretend surfing on Soul Surfer, leaping off the mini blue board to join the boys, all of them standing close and watching as Justin, *my* brother, ropes the tickets over his shoulder, Shawn helping the entire time, making sure Justin gets each and every last one, shouting *How'd you do it* as the tickets keep pouring out. Even with their cups of tokens, no matter how many times they tried, the other kids couldn't do what my brother's just done, winning big like Baba did that morning he showed up with money spilling from his pockets, proud.

I bump through the crowd that keeps growing around my brother, who looks over at me and Shawn with his eyes lighting up.

Standing between them, I loop my arms around their shoulders, bringing my brothers close so that now their faces are touching mine. The three of us laughing, shocked at how much we've just won, to the point where maybe, Shawn tells us, they're going to make us give some of it back.

With our arms tangled and knees bumping into one another's, the three of us stumble and march to the prize stand. After Justin buys us each our own stick of cotton candy, I ask what he's going to do with the leftover tickets.

He shrugs his shoulders, nibbling on his treat when suddenly he leans back, tells me to c'mon, he has an idea. I follow him through the arcade and it's as if he's leading me through a maze. We duck around the different games and stations until he finds who he was looking for. The kid who played before him, who had lost most of her tokens trying to hit the jackpot, she was the reason why the grand prize had reached up to 387. Now she's sitting in a booth all by herself, one hand picking at her freckled face, the other curling her brown hair. Handing the girl the extra tickets, Justin tells her there's still enough to get that lollypop on the top shelf she told him she wanted, the one that's as big as the moon.

On my way out Maman stops me by the door, tells me it's getting late, she doesn't want me leaving the apartment. I ask Maman to stop joking, that it's not even dark yet. Doesn't matter, she tells me. She wants me to stay home tonight.

During the day, whenever Baba's here I've learned to lie on the spot, coming up with excuses, like grabbing the key off the hook and saying Maman asked me to check the mail, or carrying out the trash to the dumpster and instead knocking on Johnny's door, telling him to come over in ten minutes to ask my dad if I can hang outside.

But with Maman I've never had to lie. Either she isn't home or she's too busy catching up on bills or whatever else to notice what I'm up to, she's never made any kind of rules about having to stay inside, definitely not on the weekend.

There's a softness in Maman's eyes and I can't tell whether she's being serious or not. You're always going to their apartment, she says. Maman tells me that it's rude spending so much time in Cynthia's home when I have a home of my own.

What's the problem with *our* apartment? she asks, and then continues, smiling, her tea-stained teeth showing. The four of us can be together tonight, she tells me, her shift got called off.

I let her know Johnny's waiting for me, that Cynthia offered to take me with them to dinner. Maman repeats herself, that she won't allow me to go, now saying it a little more seriously.

I take off my shoes and throw them into the corner, walking away from Maman and into the bathroom, slamming the door shut and sitting on the floor.

You can see him in the morning, she says, her voice soft. We'll watch a movie together, she tells me, and I'll let you choose what kind of pizza we should order.

Once the movie's credits start rolling up the screen, my brothers jump from the sofa onto the floor next to me, shaking my shoulders and pinching me.

He's such a faker, Justin says, squeezing my cheeks.

We can totally see you grinning, Shawn says, laughing on, burying his fists into my chest. Get up already and let Maman go to bed, he says into my face.

But I keep my eyes shut, trying my best not to crack, pretending I fell asleep when *Basic Instinct* finally ended, the movie Shawn said we definitely had to watch.

Maman tells my brothers she still doesn't know who the real murderer was. Was it really the doctor, she asks Justin, who like Maman liked the movie so much, the two of them agreeing there wasn't a single boring moment, or his new girlfriend?

The new girlfriend, my brother answers, that's why at the end she had the ice pick with her near his bed.

Bechareh, Maman says, feeling sorry for the character played by Michael Douglas, who I think Maman's fallen in love with. His shiny skin and thick hair, his sharp nose and dimpled chin . . . Doesn't he look Persian? she asked me and my brothers over and again.

And in the scenes when they were in bed, naked, she told us to cover our eyes, but of course we peeked through our fingers, wanting to know what having sex looks like. Sitting with Maman throughout the movie felt more like she was our older sister rather than mom, showing us a movie she said would never be allowed to play in Iran.

But by the end, I don't want to be in my bed alone. I want to stay next to Maman, close. To hold her hand the way she let me at the end of the movie, where I ran the tips of her nails in circles across my palm. I loved the way it calmed me, tickling just the tiniest bit.

Let him stay, she tells my brothers, who finally leave me alone and go to bed without me. After they're gone I bury my face into Maman's lap, and I tell her I didn't like the movie.

It was just acting, she tells me, saying not to worry. Not a real story, Maman promises.

If it was fake then how come you liked it so much?

You're supposed to be asleep, she says, touching a finger to my lips, remember? Your brothers will come back if they hear you.

I reach for Maman's hand again, but this time she stands from the floor and tells me she's going to stay up a little longer, she still has work to do. She tucks the blanket up to my chin, promising me that next time I'll get to choose the movie.

It must be early when Baba stumbles through the hallway into the kitchen. Maman sits up from the floor. I don't know if she knows I'm awake but I keep my eyes closed and hope

Baba doesn't notice me. He doesn't bother turning on any lights, so she reaches over to switch on the lamp beside us.

Baba's muttering something about lost money, opening and shutting cabinets, then turns on the tap to pour himself a glass of water. He comes and sits on the sofa in the living room, his eyes staring at the wooden shelf where Maman keeps the crystal glasses she uses for tea, brought out only for special occasions.

For a long time there is silence, until Maman looks at Baba and tells him he has to stop leaving us for days at a time and burning away the little money we have.

Baba leans the side of his face against his closed fist, for a moment shutting his eyes. He breathes in deep, sighing out loud.

So many companies looking for your experience, why won't you apply? Maman asks, her voice low and soft. Baba doesn't say anything back and I'm wishing Maman would stop. Can't she see that Baba's tired? She can talk to him tomorrow.

Baba pulls his body up straight, and as I watch him through the tiny slits between my eyelids I can tell he's spent another night without sleep, his eyes wanting to close in on themselves.

When Maman turns her back and goes to the kitchen, Baba notices me for the first time. He yanks me off the floor by my arm, tells me to go wake my brother, to tell Shawn that he needs to grab Maman's things, throw them outside. Baba says he's tired of this, tired of all of us.

Boro, he yells, the thick vein running down his forehead. Take her things and put them on the street.

Tears rush up into my eyes, stuck on Baba's words.

Maman returns to the living room, asking me to help her pick up the blankets from the floor. We're folding them when Baba walks up to her and grips her by the shoulders, hard, the first time I've seen Baba do this.

Maman doesn't move, doesn't even flinch, not until Baba shoves her into the cabinet and causes the crystal glasses to come crashing down. Maman nudges me out of the way, telling me to climb on top of the sofa, to keep my feet away from the floor as Shawn walks into the living room, sleepy-eyed, looking at the mess Baba's made.

Was there an earthquake again? he asks, scared, and Baba stays quiet. He keeps his head tilted down, the crystal glasses cracked on the floor, my brother realizing now it wasn't an earthquake that caused the loud crash.

Maman leans against the wall, her arms crossed. She's the only one who doesn't look afraid, as though she knew this was how things would go. And not only today but maybe Maman's known all along, even back when Baba had his job and we had a house of our own, a kitchen with a big white stove where Maman and I would stand together, saffron and butter filling the air as she showed me how to prepare Persian rice by dipping her finger into the pot of basmati, using the ridges on her knuckle to keep measure. The water needs to be this high, Maman would tell me, tilting the pot so I could watch, and I would pretend I didn't see it, what was right there deep inside. The promise she held on to, that our lives would get better, she looked so certain of it.

Maman stayed. It was Baba who left, and this time he was gone the entire week so that on Friday instead of going to mosque after school with my brothers, I got to be with Johnny.

With a room waiting for them at Caesars Palace, Johnny and I helped his mom and her new boyfriend carry bottles of champagne and wine into the car as they loaded their small suitcases. She planted a big kiss on his cheek, and then one on mine, too, before handing Johnny forty dollars for the weekend, for food, for whatever he wanted to do.

He came over to be with us last night, he and Justin playing Super Mario until almost midnight while me and Shawn watched. I didn't want him to leave, it felt so good having Johnny in our room all to ourselves. I didn't even care that I didn't get a turn, I was happy just to be in my bunk, watching.

And before going to sleep I put my shorts and T-shirt and even my shoes at the end of my mattress, wanting to make sure I'd be ready as soon as I woke up. Johnny promised this time he'd be up early, told me to meet him outside our building at eight o'clock sharp. He didn't say for what and I didn't bother asking.

But he won't be down for another hour, and it's too early to knock on his door and anyways I promised I wouldn't

bother him before he was ready. I leave our apartment building, figure if I walk to the mosque there'll be tea in the big
thermos on the table, and leftover dates, for the dedicated
Muslims who come for Fajr prayer, finishing their namaz just
as the sun starts its way up into the sky.

The three lanes on each side of Sherman Way are mostly
empty right now, so that the few people who are out driving
get to speed and swerve through the wide empty street, their
windows lowered with music blasting, waking themselves
and the neighborhood up. I cross to the long center divider,
looping through the palm trees planted for miles and miles,
cleaning off my dirty Filas in the damp grass.

When I cross into the parking lot and see the imam standing in the mosque doorway, dressed in his light gray prayer
gown with a Qur'an in his hand, I worry he'll ask me to join
him as he sits with others to read and recite the surah's pas-
sages. Instead of going inside I loop around the building,
wasting time.

There's an extra room attached to the back and through
a small window I see a bed the size of mine, big enough for
only one body. Where the imam lives, I guess, though it
makes me feel bad for him. His days spent in this old building and then having to sleep here, too . . . Doesn't he want to
have more than just this? Because that's what Baba's told us
when he's shared his stories of living in New York, that the
real way to get to know God is by seeing the world, meeting
people different from yourself.

We're sitting at Denny's in a dark-red booth by the window, sunshine pouring through and lighting up the shiny

top of the table. Johnny's eyes still adjusting to the morning, sleepy-faced, he orders a coffee from our waitress.

How'd you know I've been wanting to come here? I ask him, sipping from a glass of ice-cold water.

I can't believe your parents haven't brought you here before, he says, pouring sugar into his coffee, lots of it. He slides over the small dish of creamers, tells me to add as many as I'd like. My mom drinks it black but that's fucking gross. His face cringes.

I unpeel two packets of creamer and pour them into his mug, watching the coffee turn light brown as Johnny swirls his spoon inside. He tells me to add another. He takes a sip, again shakes his head. Just *one* more, he says. Now slurping on it loud, he closes his eyes and lets the coffee swish around his mouth. Delicious, he whispers, his face already a tiny bit brighter. With the sweet smell of the caramel-colored coffee when he passes the mug over to me, even before I try it I know I'm going to love it.

Johnny puts the money Cynthia gave him underneath a sticky jar of syrup on the side of the table, two twenty-dollar bills, setting it there as a reminder that we have enough money to order whatever we want.

Isn't that supposed to last you the weekend? I ask.

Doesn't matter, he tells me. We gotta make your first time count.

Flipping through the menu of different kinds of omelets and pancakes, pictures of crispy hash browns and puffy scrambled eggs, I ask him, Is it good? pointing to the strips of glistening bacon.

Hold up, he says. You've *definitely* had bacon before.

When the waitress comes back to our table, Johnny doesn't hesitate. He orders two Grand Slams for us, asking for the eggs to be cooked sunny-side-up, and when she asks whether we want bacon or sausage, Johnny pauses, looking at me.

Both, I say.

We'd like to have both, Johnny repeats to our waitress.

Should be right out. She smiles, reaching for our menus.

I think of what I'm going to have to say later tonight, when I ask God for forgiveness for eating pig even though I know it's haram.

I look past Johnny and around the restaurant, making sure nobody from the mosque is here to stop me before I have the chance to at least try it. It's delicious, Johnny says, you'll love it.

And he must be right because practically everyone here at Denny's has it on their plate. And based on how good the sizzling pork makes the restaurant smell, I believe him.

Right before lunchtime at 11:45, the school's PA system clicks on and my name crackles through its raspy speakers. It's the main office summoning me out of class, but I continue on with my assignment, pretending I don't notice it's me they're calling for.

Now Ms. Kim walks over to my desk, says that I need to pack my things and go, they're waiting for me.

In the main office Baba doesn't notice when I walk in, he's standing with his back toward me at a table in the corner, running his fingers along a globe.

Here he is, says the parent coordinator who made the announcement. Then, because Baba isn't listening, she repeats it again, louder this time, standing up from her chair and leaning forward. Sir, she raises her voice, your son. Baba turns around, a small smile on his face when he sees me.

As we walk to the car, which he parked right out front, Baba won't tell me why he's here or where he's been or why he pulled me from class. An emergency, is all he says as he unlocks the door.

Sitting at the wheel he stares out into the street, biting down on the tip of his finger. Then the lunch bell rings, snapping us out of our quiet and that's when Baba looks into my eyes, as though he's getting ready to pass on a secret. But all he does is sigh, turning the key in the ignition, looking back out onto the street as the engine trembles, vibrating my seat.

You'll see for yourself, Baba finally says. Then you can tell your brothers why the four of us are leaving.

When we pull into the parking lot of Maman's college, Baba tells me he's organized a trip for me and him and my brothers. A chance for all of us to clear our heads, Baba tells me. And when Maman realizes how much she misses us, Baba promises, she'll come join us. It'll be just like before, he says, like when we used to go camping, only this time it'll be longer than a few days.

I turn to ask Baba where we'll be going, but I stop myself because of how the muscles in his jaw tense as he bites down onto his lips, reminding me of how I'm not supposed to ask questions.

So I stay quiet, letting Baba lead the way from the parking lot.

We cut through the college campus where the buildings look new and the walkways are clean, the bushes neatly trimmed. The soccer field's as big as my school. When we get to the main quad, where Baba says we'll find Maman, I stop following him, instead watching a group of guys on the lawn tossing a Frisbee back and forth. As one of them comes sprinting toward me I stand in place, not moving. He isn't wearing a shirt, and his black-tinted sunglasses are wedged within the top of his curly fro. He leaps up into the air and reaches high with his outstretched palm, catching the Frisbee with one hand, landing just a few yards away from me as he fires it back. The smell of freshly mowed grass lingers. I reach down to pick up his sunglasses that dropped to the ground.

I go to hand them back and I keep my eyes on his stomach, where there are two veins running down to his waist, beneath his shorts.

Good looking-out, little man, he says, tapping me on the shoulder as my face turns red. He sprints back to his group and I wish he would come back to where I got to see, up close, the hairs on his chest gleaming with sweat.

Didn't you hear me calling for you? Baba yells when I catch up to him across the lawn. Why did you stop?

I mumble about the dropped sunglasses that needed to be returned, and as I apologize to Baba I try to hide the smile on my face, hiding how happy I am to have been that close to someone so handsome and tall, where for a moment it reminded me of how it feels to be around Johnny, warm in my body.

I follow Baba to the campus cafeteria, crossing through dozens of students pouring out, holding trays of food with their backpacks slung over their shoulders.

There she is, I tell Baba, pointing out Maman at one of the tables. Her textbooks splayed in front of her, she's pouring herself a cup of tea from the thermos she packs every morning, and a man half Baba's age is sitting beside her.

She looks up as if she could sense me standing here, a small smile on her face. She isn't wearing her hijab and there's makeup on her eyes.

Mary, the man calls Maman, taking off his glasses and setting down his pen. There's somebody here for you. Maman closes her notebook and nods, her smile gone.

Baba walks away, as though Maman asked him to bring me here, to drop me off.

Show her where we parked, Baba tells me. I'll be in the car.

He leaves me here with Maman and her friend, both of them look embarrassed and I am, too, for intruding on Maman. I want to explain that this wasn't my idea. I was at school, like her, when he pulled me out of class.

Without saying a word, she packs up her things and takes out her hijab from her bag, tying it around her head, and walks ahead of me as though she knows where Baba will be waiting.

Back in the car, as Maman sits staring out the window, Baba turns to me before starting the ignition and tells me he should have never allowed her to enroll in school, that he should have never brought her to this country.

Shawn and Justin, their arms crossed, stare out into the night as Baba drives down Sherman Way. I look at him from the middle seat, waiting for Baba to say something.

With our windows shut, the air inside feels thick, stuffy, my brothers and me are sweating. I keep picking at the torn fabric on my seat, scraping it back and peeling it off as small clouds of dust rise from the cushions underneath. It makes me smell old, the dust covering my fingers, making me smell like the strangers who must've been in this car before us, long ago.

At first when we left home Baba sat with his shoulders hunched and curved, hugging the steering wheel as he drove. But a little while after, he started to lean back in his seat, quiet.

He tells us we're going to a motel, by LAX, where we'll get to watch the airplanes as they land and take off, our first night of the trip.

The same airplanes you worked on at Boeing? I ask Baba, and he nods, his eyebrows scrunched, looking at me in the rearview mirror.

I try to sleep on our way, closing my eyes and leaning my head against Justin's shoulder, because maybe then the night will fade, but the shaking in his chest won't let me. Coming from his insides I can hear that he's scared, and that maybe I should be, too.

When we arrive at the motel, Baba parks the car and sits with his elbow against the window, his chin resting on top of his knuckles. He keeps his eyes down, his seatbelt still buckled. Slowly he's shaking his head, and then he begins to whisper, first to himself, then loud enough for me and Justin and Shawn to hear. She just needs time, Baba sighs, slamming his palm against the dashboard, scaring me.

He reaches over and clicks open the glove compartment, taking out a single cigarette. He puts it between his teeth, then pulls a tiny packet of matches from his coat.

Since when does Baba smoke? I ask Shawn, whispering into his ear as Baba strikes a match. He holds it in front of him, the flame crawling toward the tip of his thumb, and finally Baba lights the cigarette, sighing into the match and blowing out its flame.

Gray flakes from the end of Baba's cigarette break off, a small hiss as the ash lands on the sticky rim of the soda can he keeps by his arm. I pull in the smoke through my nose, making my head light then dizzy. If I keep breathing it in, maybe then I can make the night disappear, make the three of us in the back fade away. I don't want to be here anymore, I tell Justin, but my brother thinks I mean here inside the car.

I'll be just a minute, Baba says, opening his door. He tells us he's going to call our amoo and asks us to stay in the car.

For a moment Baba stands at the pay phone, his hands buried in his pockets, before sliding in the coins. The receiver is pressed into his ear as he hunches over the pay phone's silver box. I lean over Justin to open the car door.

What are you doing? Shawn asks.

I want to hear.

He's going to see you, my brother says.

I don't care, I tell him, pretending to be less scared than I am.

We'll land the day after tomorrow, Baba tells his brother in Farsi. Then, before hanging up, he says, What did I tell you? This country was going to spoil her, and it did.

II

The Islamic Republic of Iran

Reaching for our wrists they shout and they shove, faces that look dusty and worn. Bafarmayn, they repeat, insisting with quick hands and strong voices, asking us to join them inside. Men with thick mustaches like Baba's, wearing dress pants and loose suit jackets even in the heat.

When one of them reaches over and takes the luggage from Shawn's hand, my brother follows him to his car, telling me and Justin to stay close, but we can't keep up. Too much noise to focus, cars honking and alarms blaring, officers blowing their whistles as parents yank their children along, all in a rush, pulling them the same way they drag their suitcases.

It takes Baba a few minutes to notice our brother is nowhere near us, lost somewhere in the crowd, and as soon as he does Baba's yelling at Justin to go look for Shawn. Baba settles on a price with one of the shouting drivers, and the man stuffs our things into the trunk of an old dented white car.

Besheen, Baba says, slamming the door shut, telling me to wait inside. I switch between both windows, back and forth, searching for my brothers, but there are too many faces. Too many signs with Persian names and directions I can't read, and it seems as if in every huddle of sweaty men a fight will break out, though the opposite happens. Men who were shouting a moment ago now break into laughter as they're greeted by loved ones. Families hugging and kissing in the middle of the service road, a grandfather pinching the cheeks of two cranky kids who look like me, who clearly don't want to be here for the family reunions that carry on too long, as though there isn't a line of cars stuck behind, honking, people cursing. And the chaos of Isfahan airport goes on even louder than our airport back home, where everyone at least tries to follow the rules.

I give up searching for my brothers. In the back seat of the taxi my eyes begin to fill as it hits me how far I am from those mornings I had to myself in our building, racing up the staircase to Johnny's to check if he was awake yet. I look around one last time before I shut my eyes tight, listen to the shouting outside the car, waiting to hear familiar sounds of Spanish or English to prove to myself that I'm in L.A.

On the plane, when Justin and Shawn were asleep, Baba called me over from the other side of the aisle to sit in the empty seat beside him. He lifted the plastic window shade to show me the dry and brown mountains below, no different from the bowl of mountains that surrounded us back home. Then his hand reached for mine, squeezing my palm into his, promising me that here in Iran things would be better for us. I tried my hardest to believe him.

The door swings open, and there is Shawn biting his lip, Justin's face a blank. My brothers join me and Baba gets into the front of the taxi. Our driver flicks away his cigarette and takes his seat behind the wheel. Baba tells us to lower our heads and leans over to hit us each on the back of our necks, telling us to never again lose sight of one another.

When I look up Baba's eyes are red, wet—he looks just as scared as I am.

You're supposed to be brothers, he tells us, raising his hand once more, but this time our driver reaches over, gently holding Baba by his arm.

Agha toree neest, he says and pats our dad on his back. Baachan, our driver says. They're kids, he repeats, it happens all the time.

The driver looks at the three of us through his rearview mirror, smiling with his eyes. I reach for my seatbelt but there isn't one. Shawn wipes the snot from his nose and, smiling, says, I guess here they just don't care about that.

After seeing our driver's ID, the guard at the airport exit lifts the metal barrier and right away we're on a highway, a road that's mostly unpaved, no painted lines, no lanes. And now with our windows down my eyes begin to burn, the hazy thick air outside filling my mouth with the taste of burnt trash and gasoline, sticking to my gums and teeth, filling the insides of my nostrils.

The front of the taxi dips into a pothole and then another, with our driver telling Baba what a shame, look at how Iran has fallen apart. Baba asks him not to speak like that about their country but our driver keeps on. Naatars agha, he says, waving away Baba's worries like you would tiny gnats. Nobody's listening in on us, the driver says.

We merge onto Kaveh Boulevard, where ahead in the distance the traffic stops. Our driver cuts through by using the lane meant only for buses, other drivers holding down their horns and yelling out from their windows. He shifts into a higher gear, the engine underneath the dented hood stuttering as he accelerates and we're moving fast again, the taxi's small frame rattling.

The car comes to a sudden stop and my forehead slams into the driver's headrest. Baba smacks his hand onto the dash. Yavash, he shouts, yelling at our driver to be careful. But instead of keeping his distance from the car in front of us, the driver accelerates once more, the engine still stuttering, now protesting even louder as the car heaves and jerks forward.

Javooni, our driver says, shaking his head as he watches the motorbike beside us weave across, the woman riding on the back holding on with one hand, both riders without helmets, the loose end of her black hijab flowing in the fading afternoon light that is thick with smog and the smoke. Even though Baba is still hunched forward with his palm on the dash telling our driver to be careful, you can tell that this is just the way it is here in Isfahan. People finding their own way, honking and cutting and slamming on their brakes, dented metal frames crunching against one another as though it's all a normal part of driving.

Maybe being away from home for so many years, Baba's forgotten this. How the older adults his age sit behind steering wheels stuck in bumper-to-bumper traffic, cursing the young ones, remembering with a tiny spark what it's like to have it. Javooni, as our driver keeps repeating, their youth.

There's a garden of our own with tall green trees keeping us shaded and cool, with a small fountain for us to splash around in—I didn't think our grandfather's house would be this nice. Just on the other side of the solid metal gate, Isfahan's loud dirty streets wait for us. But inside, ripe figs on the ground burst through their purple and green skins, with a rich sticky sweetness filling the air. On the patio, leaning on his cane with one hand and holding a tattered Qur'an in the other, Baba's baba comes out to greet us.

Meeting the three of us for the first time, there isn't the smile I was expecting to see on his face but still, I can tell Haji Agha's happy we're here by the way he's standing calm and quiet, waiting for us to walk up the steps.

Justin's first, wrapping his arms around our grandfather's waist. Haji Agha leans down and plants a kiss on his forehead. We say hello one by one.

Naveh as bacheh shirin tareh, Haji Agha keeps repeating—still no smile but his eyes wet with tears, his hand patting Justin's hair. A grandchild is sweeter than the child, a phrase I've never heard before, but even the sound of the words feels sweet as they roll off Haji Agha's tongue.

Boro Reza, Haji Agha says, motioning for Baba to go inside, telling him to bring out the sleeping cushions from the living room.

Later, Haji Agha tells us, a very good friend will be here to have chai with us. Aval, he says, his hand on Justin's cheek as he lets out yet another yawn, first it's time to rest.

Baba sets up the cushions outside, the four of us lying down on the deck using them as pillows, except for Justin who rests his head on Haji Agha's chest and finally I see a smile on our grandfather's face. When Baba goes to move my brother away, Haji Agha waves off his son, saying it's okay, Justin can sleep however he wants.

· · ·

The only one awake, our grandfather is down in the garden, at the table underneath the fig trees. I see that he isn't alone, the guest who he said would be joining us is here. The two of them have their chairs positioned right beside the fountain, enjoying the light mist of water that the breeze brings them. They're deep in conversation, so that at first they don't notice me as I walk over from the deck.

Balanced on his lap is a small plate of fruit, and Haji Agha is peeling a cucumber when he sees me and asks how I slept.

Ah-leeeeee, I tell him, bringing my fingers together and raising them to my lips, making Haji Agha and his friend laugh as I kiss my fingers away.

Haji Agha slices the skinny cucumber into three, salting it first before offering it to us.

My childhood best friend, Haji Agha tells me, gesturing toward Agha Zadeh. The man who's been in charge of Iran's biggest airport for the past eleven years, he says.

Agha Zadeh clicks his tongue, waving Haji Agha's introduction away, and he asks my grandfather when he'll stop bringing up his work as if it's the most important thing in the world.

He nods his head and tells me I can call him Hassan. And if you don't want to, he says, we won't talk about airports anymore.

The tea, Haji Agha says, suddenly remembering and standing from his chair.

Like an older brother, Hassan tells me as Haji Agha walks into the house. I was your age when my father passed, he says, and it was Haji Agha who helped us, nobody else.

Then he asks if I know the story of my grandfather's bakery.

I shake my head.

Well, he says. Would you like to hear?

Baleh, I say. Hassan cracks open a pomegranate, the seeds falling out all at once into the bowl in his lap, like magic, without any of the bitter white skin that usually ruins the taste. He tosses a handful of seeds into his mouth, then hands me the bowl, saying it's all mine.

During the war with Iraq, Hassan begins, it was the most popular bakery in all of Isfahan. Eight years the war lasted and for every year, on the morning of Nowruz when Haji Agha started work, he didn't stop baking bread for the entire day, never did he take a break, not even for a glass of tea.

That's impossible, I say, smiling.

Telling stories again? Haji Agha asks, stepping into the garden with a basket of bread, a plate with walnuts and dates and fresh paneer, the same kind of cheese Maman eats at home.

Did you hear that? Hassan tells me, exaggerating his voice. I think the chai is calling for Haji Agha, he says, laughing and waving him away.

Hassan straightens the hair of his thin mustache, telling me he saw it with his own eyes.

And if Haji Agha didn't need to sleep, he says, I promise you, he would have kept baking for all thirteen days of the Persian New Year.

But why, I ask. Why all that bread?

Mazerat meekham, says Hassan, please excuse me. He

reaches over to grab another handful of pomegranate seeds from my bowl.

It's because of how bad things were, Hassan continues. No clean water, no supplies, people had nothing to eat.

It was Haji Agha's idea to make sure that for Nowruz every family who came asking for food would be fed.

Did everyone with a bakery do that?

Hassan shakes his head, tells me that because of what my grandfather did for the people of Isfahan, they continue to choose his bakery over the hundreds of others, and that now my amoo is making sure the bakery stays the same.

Inside Haji Agha's home the floor feels like it's made of pure rock. There isn't any carpet, just a single small beige rug with blue and red flowers bordering the sides. The house feels empty and abandoned, dark and damp like there's something rotting behind the walls. I don't know what it is but when I go to use the bathroom, I find out why.

There isn't a toilet, only a hole in the shower's slippery floor. I have to place one foot on each side, aiming and holding still, the water from below splashing up and catching me on the ankles. After I'm done, the stink of old crap sticks to my body no matter how much I wash.

And just like we did in our apartment back at home, me and my brothers share a room, only now Baba sleeps with us, too. The electricity comes and goes, so at night there isn't much we can do. After we go to bed, I can hear cockroaches crawling along the walls, hissing through the cracks, but when I tell Shawn he says I'm making it up, that cockroaches can't hiss. I hear them though, all through the night, and I feel them, too, skittering around my body, across my toes and shins. They know when we're asleep, Justin tells me in the morning after we finish namaz. He says he saw one crawling from Baba's forehead down to his eyelid, that it appeared as soon as Baba started snoring.

I squirm as he keeps on with the story. What'd you do? I ask.

Nothing, he says, picking up his prayer rug from the floor and shaking off the dust. What would you have done?

At the end of Haji Agha's block, there's a tiny corner store that sells bubble gum, firecrackers, soda, and Persian candies. When Baba's asleep I search through the pockets of his pants and coat, finding Iranian toman, enough to at least buy us each a piece of bubble gum, the kind with the tiny comic strip inside because here in Isfahan they have those, too, just like the 7-Eleven by our apartment in Canoga Park.

Baba is in the kitchen washing the breakfast dishes. I go to check the closet, where first I look through Baba's gray wool coat, nothing. I take his pants from the hanger, shaking them upside down, just a few pieces of lint fall out.

When I turn to leave our room, I notice his wallet sitting on the dresser beside his bed. My heart pounds as I take it with me into the bathroom.

I open it up too fast and the middle flap drops out, and a wad of Iranian bills falls to the floor. I stash a few in my socks, and when I put the flap back into its place, there's a black-and-white photograph I've never seen before, inside one of the wallet's clear plastic slots. I carefully remove the photograph. It's faded and torn. In the picture Baba and another man are standing together in front of a statue, surrounded by tall buildings with a huge Coca-Cola billboard above them and snow on the ground. Baba looks so young, a head full of big curly hair, and the man next to him looks even younger. His hair wavy and long, down to his neck, not a single mark or wrinkle on his face. They both look so handsome, so American.

I turn the photo around, and in Baba's own handwriting, the black ink smudged, *Times Square with David, 1981,* and before I have time to stuff it into my socks the bathroom door opens.

I hold up the photo for him to see, Look what I found. I hand Baba the picture.

I try to walk past him, but Baba grabs me by the shoulder. Where did you find this?

Here on the floor, I lie, feeling the bulge of his wallet in my pocket, hoping he doesn't notice.

Merci, Baba says gently, his hand on my cheek. It must've fallen from my wallet, he says.

He looks at the photo as if seeing it for the first time. The night of David's play, Baba says, smiling to himself.

Eshk, he tells me. That David's play was about love and at the end not one person was sitting down. Everyone in the theater was standing and clapping and crying, shouting and clapping again.

Did you do the special snap for him? I ask.

Pas chee, he says. Of course.

How come you left New York?

His voice lowers. The revolution, Baba says. Here in Iran they took Americans hostage at the embassy. Nobody in

New York wanted to hire an Iranian. I was there with a full scholarship from the shah himself, did you know that? Baba asks me. And at Columbia I finished at the top of my class, but that didn't matter. When bad things happen to America, Baba tells me, the people don't forget so easily, or at all.

He pats down his pockets, You haven't seen my wallet, have you?

I shake my head and tell him, I'll look in the room for you. I try to walk past and this time he lets me, shutting the bathroom door behind him.

n the alleyway behind Haji Agha's house, Shawn and I kick a soda can side to side, pretending we're like the boy from our favorite cartoon here, a young football player from Tehran with wavy black hair who grows up to become Iran's greatest star.

A week ago, right after we arrived, we saw our neighbors, Majid and Mohammad, playing in the alley, throwing firecrackers at the wall. Now the brothers come out to say hello, and Shawn asks if they have more.

Majid says he'll be right back.

We stuff the firecrackers into our pockets, the four of us marching through the alleyways behind Jay Street, looking for our target. Not until I step over broken glass do I realize that Mohammad is barefoot, and when I ask him why, he points over to his older brother and says he only gets to wear shoes when Majid isn't using them.

Shawn chooses a house that's three stories tall, a huge backyard to fling the firecrackers into. We check to make sure nobody is around, and there's nobody to get us into trouble. But before I light mine I tell them to look, the next house over has their window open and there's no screen.

Let's do it, Shawn says, reading my mind. But you go first.

Majid walks a few yards ahead for a head start, telling us we shouldn't, this is a bad idea.

I light the fuse and float the firecracker straight through the window and, before mine goes off, my brother does the same. We wait to watch as the smoke billows out, we hear a mother screaming and her children crying and when I look next to me Shawn is gone, sprinting down the alleyway while Mohammad and Majid sprint in the other direction. I chase after Shawn, feeling bad for what we've done. Worried, too, that the brothers are going to rat us out, tell their father what me and Shawn did, and he'll come searching the streets for us to teach us a lesson, making a big deal of it in front of the other neighbors, that me and my brothers don't belong here in Isfahan, we aren't wanted or welcome anymore.

On Jay Street I search for my brother. It feels like I'm in the center of the city, with the chaos of motorcycles and taxis, buses and bicyclists all fighting. Black smog fills the air, and I lift the collar of my shirt to cover my nose.

It's mostly older men out on the street, dressed in white prayer gowns and torn leather sandals. Stands selling small cardboard boxes of tea, jars of honey and dates, lavashak, too, me and my brothers' favorite candy. Men sit on empty milk crates behind the stands waiting for customers.

It's now noon and everything comes to a pause, the older men starting wudu by pouring water from a large plastic bottle over their arms and feet, combing through their hair and splashing water across their cheeks. They spread out their prayer rugs, bending over and onto the ground for namaz.

Up ahead I see Shawn, his head turning back and forth, looking for me.

Admit it, Shawn says to me, you were scared.

Do you think Majid and Mohammad are going to snitch on us? I ask.

I hope not, Shawn says. Baba wouldn't let us leave Haji Agha's anymore, that's for sure.

Where do you think he goes every day?

Looking for work, my brother mumbles, though the way Shawn says it, it doesn't sound like he really believes it.

Or maybe he's found a new wife, he then adds. Yeah, that's probably it, Shawn says, agreeing with himself. Fucking up our family isn't good enough for Baba, he needs another wife to keep the streak going.

Congratulations, he tells me, bumping me in the shoulder. Now you'll get to see how it feels to have a younger brother.

I'd prefer a sister, I tell him, keeping his dumb joke going. There's plenty of you and Justin to go around.

You're only saying that because you're a mama's boy, he says.

He stops walking, pausing in front of a store that sells random bundles of electronics. I'm close enough now to see a shadow of a mustache starting to grow on his upper lip.

Do you really think she's thinking about us right now? Shawn asks me. Or that she even misses us? 'Cause I don't. I bet you Maman's already moved out of our apartment, started a new life somewhere.

I tell my brother he's wrong, that of course she misses us.

Keep dreaming, he says.

On Saadi Street, we stand outside the window of Haji Agha's bakery, watching our amoo before going in. We never get to see Baba's younger brother because he's always busy here at work. A cigarette dangles from the corner of his mouth, and he smokes without ever pulling the cigarette out, somehow keeping the growing ash from breaking off. Amoo's lips are pale and cracked and his hands caked all the way up to his forearms in flour, pulling out loaves from the oven where a fire burns beneath a pile of stones.

Yesterday I came here with Baba, Shawn tells me. He said he wanted to pick up bread, and after they spoke for a few minutes, Baba started shouting at Amoo. Next door, my brother says, pointing to the beige building, Baba kept saying that part of it belongs to him.

I walk over, running my hand along the building's tall stone pillars. Above, so many bright blue tiles glazed with Persian writing decorate the entrance.

It's beautiful, I tell Shawn.

He tells me Baba thinks it's a waste of money what Amoo is doing. Using the building for a private elementary school where he doesn't charge the parents. Baba told me they could sell it and make a lot of cash. Money he says belongs to him, Shawn says.

I'm glad Amoo hasn't listened to him, I tell Shawn, and just then our uncle steps out of the bakery, surprised to see us.

Don't mention anything I said, Shawn whispers to me.

Our amoo invites us in. He clears a wooden table in the corner of the bakery, gesturing for us to sit.

He brings three glasses of tea, along with a plate of bamieh and a stack of zoolbia, gold and sticky and sweet.

How is your dad doing? he asks my brother. Shawn nods, Merci, bad neest, he tells our amoo.

Khejalat keshidam, Amoo says, apologizing for the way he behaved yesterday afternoon when Shawn and Baba visited.

Gooshkon, our amoo continues, using the wooden stick of a used match to pick through his teeth. For Haji Agha and me, he says, this place means everything. The building next door, we saved for years to buy it.

Midoonam, Amoo, Shawn says. I understand.

Divoonehs, Amoo says. Because the children are disabled the other schools call our students crazy, and they reject them. Their parents are told to keep them home, he says, turning his face away for a moment as it gets red with anger.

He looks out the window, then watches me and Shawn as we sip from our teas, dunking in sugar cubes and slurping on them.

Do you know, says Amoo, I've taught the oldest ones how to bake sangak?

Lotfan, I say. Please don't sell the building. How else will the children get to learn?

You understand, he says. No school, and then what, he asks, gorosneh? Staying hungry for the rest of their lives once their parents pass, that's what happens in this country. I don't—

Is there sangak to take back for Haji Agha? my brother interrupts.

Amoo smiles, his eyes narrowing and eyebrows rising, the way Baba's do. He stands from the table and bags three long sheets of sangak, roping them over our shoulders.

Can I come back tomorrow? I ask Amoo.

Lotfan, he says. I'd love to show you the school.

Once on the street Shawn punches me in the back, hard, knocking the air out of my body so that I drop the bread. He says he told me not to say anything about the building. If Baba finds out what you said to Amoo, Shawn shouts, it's gonna be me who he fucking hits, watch.

At Naqsh-e Jahan Square, my brothers and me sit in front of the mosque by a fountain as wide and big as a swimming pool. Haji Agha said this all used to belong to the shah.

Horses pull wooden carriages around the square, and bunches of kids circle the fountain, splashing and shouting in the mist as they chase one another, their mothers yelling for them to be careful, to stay away from the ledge.

Shawn dares Justin to ask for a free ride, pointing to a man whose skin looks like it's never taken a break from the sun. Justin skips toward the man as he leads his horse to the water. It's as if he knows what Justin's about to say, because before my brother speaks the man clicks his tongue and waves his arm in the air, gesturing toward his carriage, telling us to climb on.

Pool nadareem, Justin says, turning his pockets inside out, showing the man he doesn't have any money. Again the man says not to worry, waving away the concern on our faces.

The three of us hop on, riding in the back of the carriage, where Shawn stands with his chest out, looking over the people in the square and pretending he's the shah.

Your brother—the man turns his head to face Justin and me—he reminds me of my oldest son.

Where is he now? Justin asks.

Tell him to come sit with us, I say.

Zeereh zameen, the driver says, pointing to the ground.

Justin and I look at each other, not knowing what to say.

When we circle back to the mosque, the man points up to its blue and gold dome, the glazed tiles gleaming in the sun. He tells us about the artists who centuries ago designed the wide pillars and rows of balconies with a terrace on the top, and how in this very spot hundreds and hundreds of people would join together, gathering for sunrise prayer.

He gets quiet, as if it's him who's seeing the mosque for the first time, not us.

Will the Pahlavi family ever come back for their country? I ask.

Shawn pinches me, tells me I'm being zesht, I'm a guest and I shouldn't be so rude. Baba already told us to not bring up Iran's past, he reminds me.

Toree neest, the driver says, looking over his shoulder, nodding as another carriage driver goes past.

He leans back, closer to us, the smile gone from his face, the smell of cigarette smoke on his breath. They say it was the revolution, he tells us, but it was America that removed the shah from Iran. Ask your father, and he will tell you the story.

But that—

Our driver holds a finger against his pressed lips, again looking around him. Here in this country, he says, you shouldn't talk about these things. Have you boys eaten? he asks, changing the subject.

I tell Justin and Shawn I'm starving, my stomach jumping at the mention of food.

It's taarof, Justin says. He doesn't actually mean it, he's

just being nice. But the kind and gentle look on the driver's face says otherwise, offering us a place in his home to eat and drink chai.

Wanting to convince them, again I look over at my brothers, who seem so certain that the driver's invitation isn't one we should take. Merci, Agha, Shawn chimes in, but our dad has lunch waiting for us at home.

I watch as my brothers leap off the carriage, and for a moment I stay, consider riding farther on so that I could meet the man's family, so I can hear more about his son who's buried, why he died.

Khodafez, Justin waves, yanking my shirt.

Khodafez, I wave to the man's pretty horse as it trots away.

Shawn breaks off into a sprint toward the Qeysarie gate that leads into the Bazar Bozorg, Justin and me chasing our brother until we reach a long corridor surrounded by stores and stands, and people eating and drinking tea, bargaining for lower prices. Isfahan's Grand Bazaar is an entire neighborhood inside. The mud ceiling hangs low like a cave, a huge maze of cool and dimly lit tunnels filled with more things than my eyes can keep track of. Antiques, silver and bronze, spilling out from every corner. Metal pots and pans and crystal plates, jewelry and watches and chains, a row of wooden instruments where a man and his daughter string together a tanbur right in front of our eyes.

I see a red Persian rug hanging from a hook, the same colors and shapes as the rug Maman has back home. I run my fingers through the loose strings at the end, pulling on them without realizing it's causing the rug to come undone, fabric unwinding as the string grows and grows. An elderly man sitting on a plastic crate begins to shout, limping over with a broom. Boro gomsho, he yells, swatting me away.

I catch up with Justin and Shawn, who are waiting at the exit, only instead of leading back to the square it leads into a courtyard separate from the bazaar.

It's quieter here, a fountain in the center, birds sipping from its clean water, and at the end of the courtyard, there's a small café with a few tables. A small group of tourists smoke from hookahs, an open backgammon board in front of them.

The three of us sit and rest at one of the empty tables, sweating. I pull from my sock the bills I took from the inside pocket of Baba's wallet, flashing the money as both Justin and Shawn begin to laugh.

Where did you get that from?

I'll be right back, I say, stepping over to the café counter.

I wait until the shop owner sees me and leans over. Befarmayn, he says. What can I get for you?

Three ice creams, please.

Smiling, he asks, You three are American boys, yes?

I nod as one of the guys from the table across the courtyard walks over, joining me at the counter. Amir, he shouts out, cigar daree?

When he reaches to grab the pack of cigarettes, the top of his waist brushes against my arm and the smell of his skin, a mix of cologne and cigarette smoke and sweat, slips down and I can taste it on my lip, where I wish it would stay.

He walks back to his table and I do, too, balancing three cups of pistachio and cardamom ice cream in my hands. I want to tell Justin and Shawn that they should go, to leave me here. That way the guy can come and sit with me here, the one with the cigarette between his lips and the unbuttoned denim shirt, black curly hairs spilling from his chest.

Shawn takes one bite from his ice cream, passes the rest over to me.

I want Rocky Road from Thrifty's, he says. Not this crap.

Justin nudges my shoulder. Go ask your new friend, he tells me. A scoop of American ice cream for this precious princess over here, Justin says, pointing at Shawn.

Don't act like you don't miss it, Shawn tells him.

Justin turns to say something back, but then pauses, looking around the courtyard.

You know what I miss? Justin says. I miss being able to sleep.

Shit, I even miss school, Justin continues, forcing a smile, using the top of the small wooden spoon to trace a triangle into his ice cream.

Something I was good at, he tells us, and it made sense to me.

He points over to the fabric shop, not a single customer inside, the shopkeeper in the corner sitting on a small rug, his eyes closed, fingering a string of rose-colored prayer beads.

The people here, Justin says, all they do is pray rather than work for something.

That's what I'm saying, Shawn jumps in, his face angry.

I miss *our* country, he tells us, where we had shit to do other than pray and take naps in the middle of the day like we're in fucking preschool.

And the way they always ask us *Is America better than Iran?* Justin says, rolling his eyes.

Right away Shawn responds, yelling it from the table, the

answer he gives each time the elders in Isfahan ask. Harf nadare, Shawn says, no question about it, his face and voice imitating the older Iranians we've encountered in Haji Agha's neighborhood, as he squints his eyes and purses his lips and waves his hand in the air, making me and Justin laugh.

The metal frame of Baba's bed rattles as he snores, so that I lie here, listening, my eyes open. A small black fan in the corner circles the hot stuffy air around us, buzzing through the night.

It feels so long ago, when my brothers and I were lying next to Maman watching a movie together, feeling the tips of Maman's nails across my palm. Now I do the same with the corner of my pillow cover, folding it and using the small soft point to run across the inside of my hand, asking Maman why it's taking her so long to get to Iran, even after Baba called last week.

With her, Haji Agha's house would be less scary. With her, I wouldn't be so lonely. But Baba said Maman won't come. She wants America to herself, he told us. Thinking of her I remember Canoga Park, our building and Christian and Johnny, sitting by the staircase with them and laughing as they told their stories—but this is why Shawn made me promise to stop remembering. He knows how Baba gets when I start crying, how much I miss standing on the pegs on the back of Johnny's bike riding through the Valley on our way to the Wash, holding on to his shoulders. My eyes keep filling, I'm not able to stop them, and it gets harder and harder to breathe as if the tears have lungs of their own, taking all the air from mine. Noises stutter out from my throat lasting so long they might end up waking Baba, and if tonight it happens again, if he wakes, it'll be him who forces the memories to stop.

It isn't until he begins shouting from the other side of the room, telling Justin to go to sleep, that I realize my brother's awake, too, whispering in the quiet, asking to go back home.

Only instead of listening to Baba and making his voice stop, Justin says it again. Take us back, my brother shouts, and even Shawn turns over in his bed, begging Justin to quit making noise.

Baba's legs swing out from underneath the covers and he sits there for a moment, wiping the tired out from his eyes, sighing as the bottom of his feet press onto the floor.

He asks Justin what his problem is, if he's trying to wake Haji Agha with all his yelling. He reminds Justin that our grandfather is sick, that he needs rest, and he tells my brother to go back to sleep.

But Justin isn't afraid of Baba like I am, or maybe he is and it's just that not being able to sleep has gotten so bad that he can't take it anymore. He's kept up at night listening to the cockroaches scurrying around his pillow while thinking about how much he misses school and our room, then he's expected to be up with the sun for namaz, so that now even as our dad tells him to stop, my brother doesn't listen. He's still shouting, asking Baba why he even brought us here to begin with. We belong where we were born, he yells.

Baba reaches for his pants and removes the belt as his voice rumbles. His shadow moves across the wall and leans over Justin, who keeps on with his questions, even louder now. And as Baba lashes him I listen to my brother sobbing, lying there in his bed, loudly pulling in the snot from his nose, both he and Baba breathing hard. He hits Justin more and harder than he's ever done before, until finally he stops, unwinds the belt from his fist and tosses it into the corner on the floor. He shouts at Justin, and at me and Shawn, too, tells us he's going to the bathroom and he shouldn't hear a single sound from us when he's back.

When Baba leaves I reach to the small table where Haji Agha keeps his Qur'an, finding the mohr I saw earlier in the day, the small clay prayer stone my grandfather said I could have. I keep the stone clenched in my palm, tighter and tighter, praying for our trip in Iran to end, as the tears hiccup out of me. I tell myself that Justin's going to be okay, of course he is. Back at home he was always the first to crack a joke after Baba would hit us, even if he still had tears in his eyes. But now the way he's turned over in bed, completely silent, makes me think this time Baba did something to my brother that will leave a mark.

Go to sleep, Shawn tells me, when he hears me sniffling, and I do my best to listen to my brother, staying silent and still like him.

Turning over and facing the window, I don't let go of the stone in my palm, and I ask God to help me fall asleep before Baba gets back from the bathroom.

When I open my eyes it's the middle of the night, dark, hot. I feel Baba lift my blanket, asking me to make room as he slides half of his body in, joining me underneath the sheet. I can feel his heart pounding hard, heat rising through his skin. Whispering, Baba tells me he's here to help me sleep as he nudges me farther toward the window to make more room, my body wedged within the small space between the wall and my mattress.

I stare at the ceiling, Baba gently wipes away the trace of dried tears at the corners of my eyes. He rests his hand on my face, soft, and there's the smell of cigarette smoke, or maybe the smog of Isfahan's streets trapped deep in his skin. Bebakhshid, I whisper, telling Baba I'm sorry for making noise, and his hand inches over to cover my eyes, lowering their lids by brushing them down.

He tells me it's okay, turning me to the side so that now I'm facing the wall. Baba holds me close, his body sticky with sweat, until I stop shaking. On the other side of the room it's silent, and I try to fall asleep as Baba's hand quietly peels off my pajamas and underwear, lowering them to the backs of my knees. The air in the room is hot against my naked skin as he starts whispering in my ear, telling me not to worry— Baba's here, he says.

For a moment he lets me lie on my own as he reaches for himself, my body still. I stare into the wall's glossy yellow paint, following its reflection with my eyes until I find a deep crack, imagining that it's the same cracked stucco in the walls of our building back home even though they look nothing alike. I feel him growing, the bed creaking as Baba moves what's now hard between my bottom, stretching me, his breath growing faster, hotter, wet on my neck. My palms and the bottom of my feet are freezing, letting out icy sweat, but on the inside it begins to burn, my stomach on fire as Baba rubs himself against me. I want to tell him to stop, that I promise I'll fall asleep, but then he'll shout at me and my brothers will wake and see what Baba and me are doing. They'll say this is the reason why I've always been his favorite.

So instead I stay quiet, the crumbly skin on my lips glued together and I press down hard into the bottom of my teeth. Baba's voice in my ear, saying this is good for me, it's going to help me sleep. And so I do my best to drift away, remembering the time I sat on Baba's shoulders in the ocean, how much better it was that he disappeared below. Leaving me in the lap of the wave, everything around me so still and blue, and with my eyes shut I'm there again. In Malibu's shadowy water not needing my brothers or Baba or even Maman, where my body is mine, only mine, as another wave comes crashing down all around me.

Baba takes my hand and puts it between my legs where it's warm and sticky, wet. Pesaram, he whispers, once this happens for you, that's when you'll know you've become a man, Baba tells me.

I watch as he stumbles from my bed to the other side of the room. When he's far enough I reach down to pull up my underwear, using it to wipe myself clean. I hide it beneath my mattress, where I won't ever touch it again.

Azizam, Maman whispers, wake up.

I'm here, my dear, she keeps repeating, running the back of her finger along my cheek. Her lips hovering over my ear, softer now. Azizam, she says, it's time to go. Time to wake up.

My hands are tucked into my chest and my body curled, lying on the deck in Haji Agha's yard. For as long as I can I pretend to be asleep. The cool breeze settles in, the sun is starting to go down, which means any minute now Haji Agha will wake from his nap and now that Maman is here we'll all be together.

I let the summer evening soak and spread the sweetness of Maman's voice, wondering if they can hear it the way I do, how Maman's words have only soft edges, how when she speaks the soot and the smell of gasoline in Isfahan's air disappears.

My eyes pinch shut, I don't want Maman to see how much I've missed her as again she whispers, It's okay, azizam, wake up.

I inhale the familiar smell of cardamom and rock sugar as Haji Agha brings out tea, the sweetness of figs falling from the trees. And even as I try to keep them sealed my eyelids open on their own. I'm awake, Maman, I'm awake, I want to shout, but when I open my eyes I see a face that looks only a little bit like Maman's, but with her exact voice.

It takes me a second to realize it's Maman's sister, our khaleh, who we've only ever seen in photographs, all the way here from Tehran though no one told us she'd be here when we woke up.

Salaam azizam, Khaleh says, tears in her eyes. Her hair and her skin lighter than Maman's, her face long instead of round, and when I close my eyes and listen to Khaleh's voice, it really does feel like Maman is here.

Lifting me up into her arms, Khaleh tells me she came as soon as she could after Maman called to let her know me and my brothers were here. And though Baba says I'm too big to be held she continues holding on to me. My cheek rests against her warm shoulder as we walk out.

My brothers follow behind, stumbling out from the wooden gate. Justin, wiping the tears from his face with the back of his wrist, keeps repeating to Khaleh that he wants Haji Agha to come with us.

You'll be back after the weekend, Baba says, speaking for Khaleh.

Her white sedan with its broken A/C sputters out warm air, but I don't care. With Khaleh, inside her car, Isfahan is better.

I have a surprise for you, she tells us, backing out of the driveway, then shifting into first gear, the engine revving as the car climbs up the hill.

Instead of turning onto Jay Street, Khaleh takes the back roads, alleyways and dark streets, the part of the neighborhood Shawn and I came to with Majid and his brother when we didn't want to be seen.

Taking Kaveh Boulevard all the way, Khaleh drives for

fifteen minutes and finally there it is, to our right, what our aunt wanted to show us, the Khaju Bridge, which me and my brothers have only seen during the day, while in the car with Baba quickly driving by it. Now there's a glow of rich golden light coming from the bridge's archways, more archways than I can count patterned across the night sky.

Khaleh pulls to the side of the road, next to a park. I know it's late, she says, but for just a few minutes, how about we go and see it up close.

This was my favorite place to come when I lived here in Isfahan, Khaleh tells us as we walk across the bridge.

With Maman? I ask, and Khaleh nods. She watches as crowds of people walk back and forth, some gathering to pose for pictures. And as she quietly smiles to herself, I can tell Khaleh's remembering back to being with her sister. Coming here on their own to spend time together, she and Maman must've been close, way closer than I feel to my brothers.

Once we reach the huge pavilion at the center of the bridge, Khaleh points up to the ceiling of the dome, showing us the beautiful paintings and tiles, the calligraphy etched into the clay and brick walls. She tells us about Shah Abbas, who had this bridge built centuries ago, and how the shah himself would come to this very spot, just as we are now, to enjoy the view of Isfahan.

Pointing down to the dried-up riverbed, I ask Khaleh where all the water has gone.

There isn't enough, Khaleh explains, so here they shut it off, save it and use it for other cities.

But even without the water that's supposed to be underneath the bridge, it's as though all of Isfahan has come here tonight, enjoying the view from the surrounding parks. There are kids younger than us running in the grass as their parents lay out a picnic of tea and fruit and sunflower seeds, groups of friends play cards and elderly men with backgammon boards set out before them. Everyone is together, shoulder to shoulder on the grass, drinking tea and smoking hookah, laughing. It's the middle of the week but nobody seems to be paying any attention to how late it's getting.

That's the way we are. No matter how much they take from us, Khaleh says, closing her eyes and breathing in the air that no longer seems so bad—we find a way to enjoy.

Enjoy *what?* says Shawn, covering his eyes with his T-shirt as the wind kicks up dust and dirt from the empty riverbed. Zendegi, Khaleh emphasizes, turning to face us. We still have this life to enjoy, she says, wouldn't you agree?

For almost five hours straight, we drive through the dark desert, nothing else, my brothers asleep and snoring in the back seat. Only once we stop to refill on gas, and while Khaleh waits for the pump to finish I join her outside.

It was you who Haji Agha was talking to this morning? I ask her, remembering how after breakfast he spent almost an hour on the phone, which he rarely ever uses. Is that why you came to Isfahan for us?

Khaleh shakes her head, looking out toward the desert, the dusty dark sky. Your maman asked me to, she tells me, and again Khaleh's eyes begin to shine with tears. Is it true? Khaleh asks. You and your brothers, you didn't know he was bringing you to Iran?

I shake my head. Baba told us we would be home after a few nights, I tell her.

Khak ba saresh, Khaleh whispers, her face angry. He should be ashamed of himself, she says. Such beautiful boys and this is what he does?

But I don't know how to answer Khaleh back, what to say to her, because nobody's ever spoken about me and my brothers like this, and it surprises me as she says how much she loves us, promising to take care of me and Justin and Shawn, her eyes and her voice rising, strong.

Back in the car as Khaleh focuses on the road in front of her, I stare out my window. It's pitch black, not like L.A. where there are streetlights guiding the way. But Khaleh doesn't seem nervous, or scared. She says she's made this drive a thousand times, she could practically do it with her eyes closed, until finally, Tehran stretches out in front of us, lighting up the nighttime sky.

At her apartment our aunt already has a place for us to sleep set up in the living room, and unlike Haji Agha's there aren't any cockroaches or cracked walls, no underground smells. I turn over to ask Justin if he's okay, but both of my brothers are already deep into sleep, gone for the night. After another hour of trying my hardest to ignore the sounds coming from Khaleh's kitchen, the clanking of pipes and the refrigerator's quiet hum, making me worry that somehow it's Baba who's here, waiting for me to drift off so he can join me on the floor—I stand up and bolt into her room.

Azizam, she whispers, sitting up in bed as if she was expecting me. Is everything okay?

I can't sleep, I say, wiping away my tears. There's someone hiding in the kitchen waiting for me to fall asleep.

Come, she tells me, lifting up her blanket and tucking me inside, my head resting on her chest. Then, once my body is still, she says, Can I show you something?

She gets up, putting on her night robe and switching on the light. Follow me, she whispers, and with Khaleh's blanket draped over my shoulders and head, I walk with her into the kitchen. She switches on the light, waits until I raise my eyes.

See, Azizam, she whispers. There's nobody here.

Down there, I tell her, pointing underneath the sink.

Together we search, opening the cabinets, checking the kitchen's closet.

All gone? asks Khaleh.

He'll come back.

Not while you're with me, she promises.

Since we're already up, Khaleh says, how about you help me make tea?

As we wait for the water to boil, Khaleh pulls down a book she keeps on the shelf above the stove, asking if Maman has ever read Farrokhzad for us.

I shake my head, asking Khaleh what a *Farrokhzad* is.

She lets out a loud quick laugh, covering her mouth and then covering mine because I start laughing as well. *Shh*, she says, we're going to wake your brothers.

After we both are quiet again, Khaleh tells me that Forough Farrokhzad was one of Iran's most important poets, and Khaleh's favorite ever since she was in high school.

I'll read you one of her poems, Khaleh whispers. But this will be only for us, okay?

I bring one finger to my lips, like the man on the carriage from Naqsh-e Jahan Square, and Khaleh begins.

On the cover there's a photograph of Forough, looking straight at me. Her head slightly tilted to the side, short black hair hugging her ears. The top corner of Forough's mouth lifts in the smallest way forming a tiny smile, but maybe it's her eyes—eyes that are dark, almost black and still shining, as though there are tiny coals lit beneath them, burning bright—that make it seem like Forough is smiling.

And her poem, too, as though her words live deep inside her eyes, words that Forough says are sparked by life, the page glowing beneath her fingers.

Do you know what I want of life? Khaleh reads, *that I can be with you, you, all of you—*

The kettle whistles loudly, startling both me and Khaleh. When she stands to turn off the stove, the question comes out on its own.

Khaleh, I say. Is Maman a little like Forough?

She turns around, now looking straight into my eyes.

How do you mean, Khaleh asks softly.

Maman wants something else, I say.

Khaleh takes in a deep breath, sitting back down beside me, resting her chin on her fist. For a moment we both watch as the tea steeps in her glass, the water becoming golden red.

Khaleh holds my face in both palms, her hands warm, she kisses me on my cheek before lifting me onto her lap even though I'm too big to fit, my face resting on her chest. I can feel her heart beating hard, slow. Khaleh takes small sips from her tea, offering me the glass.

Naa merci, I tell her.

Then she starts, her voice like it was when she was reading Forough's poem, strong, low—I can see it like it was yesterday, Khaleh tells me. I went to Saadi Street to buy bread at Haji Agha's bakery, and everyone there was spreading the news. Haji Agha's son was coming back from America, the successful engineer who made a life for himself there. He was coming home to find a wife, they said.

He came looking for Maman? I ask.

Khaleh clicks her tongue. Here the tradition is different, Khaleh explains. First, he had to come over for tea.

Khaleh stares down into her glass before continuing.

He was wearing a handsome gray suit, his face freshly shaved and as he spoke to Baba-jan he never looked away from Maryam.

What was he saying?

Telling us about his life in America, Khaleh says. The houses he owned, his job as an engineer and the reputation he built for himself. We all listened and didn't say a word. We all believed him.

I don't want Khaleh to stop telling me the story of how Baba was before my brothers and I came, how he arranged his marriage to Maman, stories they've never told us before.

I remember how happy she was, Khaleh continues, how after your father came back for the second time, Maryam-jan said yes, she would marry him, she wanted to go to America.

Because it's better there, I say, looking up at Khaleh.

Khaleh nods. Yes, because in your country, she tells me, her voice becoming a whisper again, Maryam has permission to do what she wants.

I'm about to tell Khaleh that isn't true, with Baba things

are different, but then I remember how it was Maman who started training as a nurse's assistant, never telling us about it until she was done, until she found a job and then started going to college as well. It was Maman who said she was going to earn her license to get better work at the hospital, more responsibilities than cleaning patients, to earn more money.

It's what she always wanted, Khaleh says. Ever since Maryam-jan was little, always she would say, *One day I'm going to leave and never come back.*

To a place where she could have a new life, Khaleh adds, standing from the table and rinsing her glass in the sink.

And a new name, I think to myself, remembering what her classmate had called Maman.

How about you, Khaleh-jan. Will you always live by yourself? I ask.

She looks around her kitchen, thinking to herself.

I like it here by myself, she tells me. You're not worried about me, are you?

But won't you get married like Maman did?

Azizam, she whispers, running the back of her hand over my face, letting out a big breath. How do I say this, she whispers, drifting off into her own thoughts.

Khaleh tells me, The person I love—we wouldn't be able to get married even if we wanted to.

She closes the book, snapping it shut and putting it back on the shelf.

Tomorrow we'll finish the poem, she promises. We still haven't slept yet, remember?

We're supposed to leave Tehran on a Monday, to be back at Haji Agha's after the weekend. When he calls in the morning we're all sitting in the kitchen, just about to eat breakfast. Scrambled eggs with cherry tomatoes and green onions, a basket full of hot bread. Khaleh has tea on the stove, steeping.

The three of us agree to take turns speaking to our grandfather on the phone, and as I wait for mine, I play with the dial, sticking my finger into each of the digit's holes, turning it and watching for what will happen.

Justin speaks to Haji Agha the longest, and halfway through their conversation I lean closer and closer to the phone, worried I won't get my turn, listening as our grandfather explains that we'll be staying with our aunt a while longer. She's going to take us to Shomal, he tells Justin, where we'll get to see Iran's beauty, the high mountains, so much green.

Justin nods as he listens to Haji Agha, then hangs up instead of passing the phone to me.

He had to go, my brother tells me.

Did you ask about Baba? I ask.

He's working, is all Haji Agha said.

We get to Shomal late in the afternoon. Even though it's warm outside, it's raining, sheets and sheets that won't stop falling. Khaleh brings us to a house in the middle of a forest, surrounded by oak trees and maple trees, big green mountains in the distance. The air is clean and I tell Khaleh I never want to leave, that it even smells like there's an ocean nearby.

The Caspian Sea, she tells us, breathing the air deep into her lungs, smiling.

She shows us our room, tells us we can nap while she's getting dinner ready or, if we want, go outside and explore. The house has big wide windows and warm wooden floors, there's even a fireplace.

We tell Khaleh we'll be back, and leaving the house me and my brothers take the wet road to wherever it'll go. Eventually, we come across a school, and it looks nothing like ours back home. The school here in Shomal has one main room without a door or glass windows and no floors. It is made of mud and stone. They don't have tetherball or soccer or basketball courts, no monkey bars and swings. Students sit in front of a dusty chalkboard pretending to listen. They watch me and my brothers as we walk past, and I imagine myself in one of their seats.

The road continues winding into Shomal's jungle of trees. We hear running water, maybe a stream, and Justin goes searching for it.

About five minutes later he yells out, telling us to hurry, and when we reach Justin he already has his shirt stripped off, standing on top of the highest boulder. The river is wide and it looks deep, and I don't believe he'll actually jump but he does, leaping from the rock into the water. The second Shawn looks away I push him in. I join my brothers in the river as the three of us dunk ourselves under, shooting our bodies into the air by kicking up from the muddy bottom.

This is heaven, Shawn says, making his body weightless as he floats on his back. Try it, he tells Justin and me, just let go and it'll work.

My brothers' eyes are closed, the three of us listening to the collection of sounds coming from birds somewhere high in the trees.

It's like music, Justin says, opening his eyes and searching up into the sky. Running across his chest and the top of his neck he still has the bruises from Baba's belt, welts that look like they want to bleed.

Does it hurt? I ask. He shakes his head. Not anymore, he says, and now Shawn opens his eyes, too.

Let's stay in Shomal forever and never go back to Baba, I say to my brothers as I stand, scooping handfuls of water and dumping them over my head, feeling, each time I shut my eyes, that the water is washing away everything.

Shawn nods and promises, This is our new home. He smiles before diving underneath. Justin and I follow along, swimming after our brother as we try and catch up, the three of us flowing downstream.

On Friday, the holiest day of the week, when every store and restaurant and office is closed, Khaleh drives us back to Tehran. This time, though, we don't go to her apartment, she drives us straight to Mehrabad International Airport, pulling to the side just before the entrance.

Why are we here? Justin asks from the back seat.

She turns to him and Shawn, and then me. You are going back home, Khaleh says.

The three of us are quiet, looking at one another, then back to Khaleh.

You mean to L.A.? Shawn finally says.

Areh. Khaleh nods.

Justin's knees begin to shake, seems like he might open the door and start racing toward the terminal.

But Baba said we had to stay here in Iran, I say, scared that Khaleh's made a mistake, that once we're inside the security guards will make us leave the airport, that they won't let us get on the plane no matter how badly we want to, not without our dad's permission.

You remember Agha Zadeh? Khaleh says. He and Haji Agha arranged everything, and again she starts to drive, entering the airport. It's time you boys went home to Maman, she says.

Khaleh pulls to the curb and, outside, waiting for us like she said he'd be, I recognize Agha Zadeh right away, our grandfather's childhood friend, standing by the terminal. Opening our door for us, he helps Khaleh unload our bags from the trunk. His dark brown eyes have a shine in them, just like Khaleh's, who now looks away from us, covering her mouth with the end of her hijab.

When Agha Zadeh hands her the envelope with our tickets inside, she doesn't say a word.

Your mother is going to be so happy to see you three, Agha Zadeh says.

Khaleh walks us to the gate, Agha Zadeh trailing behind. Before walking through the security check, he hands me a backpack stuffed with Persian treats—nuts and dried fruit and lavashak. For when you get home, he says, to remember Iran.

When the officer asks us where we're coming from, and why, Shawn does the talking, repeating what Agha Zadeh told him he would need to say. That we were visiting our grandfather for the summer, our first time in Iran.

Even as the officer tries confusing Shawn, asking him question after question in a voice that makes it seem like we've done something wrong, Shawn keeps his face straight, never flinching, answering with the same response each time. We're American citizens, he tells the officer, who continues examining our passports.

Then it's three loud thumps with the stamp, and when I look to see what the pages read, the date of our arrival is marked in a deep bold pink.

AUG 22, 1994, the day before my tenth birthday.

I reach out to grab the corner of Shawn's jersey, twisting it around my finger, worried that if I let go, I'll get left behind underneath the white lights that are too bright for my eyes, left with the strangers crossing our path, going this way and that way, abandoned with the voices spilling from speakers up too high to find.

It's me who sees her first as we pinch our bodies through. Maman standing by the glass door at the end of the terminal, just as we were told she would be. She's waiting for us in the crowd, her arms crossed. She has on a white sleeveless blouse and her hair is shorter, like Forough's, down to her ears. In the last three months maybe me and my brothers have changed just as much.

The suitcase I'm rolling drops from my hand, smacking against the shiny tile floor, and it makes Maman smile, the way I'm sprinting toward her. Her hand is now on my chin as she brings my face against hers, Maman's palm is so soft on my face, her skin both warm and cool. I want to tell her about Iran all at once. Meeting her sister, going to Shomal, floating in the river with Justin and Shawn.

Salaam, Maman, says Justin, wrapping his arms around her, squeezing tight, and even Shawn is happy to see her, stuffing down a grin.

She helps with the suitcases and now we're outside, met by the soft early night, the gentle swoosh of air brushing against my face.

Down the sidewalk the taxis are lined up. Maman gets in first. The three of us stand outside, and she asks what we're waiting for. Zoodbash, she says, I'm going to be late for work.

On the 405 Freeway Maman finds out the driver's from Shiraz and she's asking him all these questions, saying it was always too far for her to visit when she lived in Iran. I want to tell Maman I understand every word she's saying, to show her how much my Farsi has improved after being in Isfahan.

Doesn't he look like our amoo, I say to Shawn, and that's when I start pretending our driver is one of us, that he's our uncle. We pass underneath one green billboard and then another, their silver letters shining in the night, names starting to look familiar. Because our driver is now part of our family, I start to tell him what it was like in Isfahan.

Agha Taxi Driver, I whisper, me and my brothers rode behind a horse through the square that once belonged to the shah, and we watched Isfahan's golden blinking lights from the Khaju Bridge, too. We're real Iranians now, I whisper as he takes the exit at Sherman Way.

A row of lights line the street, orange pouring into the taxi. Palm trees reach up as if they're trying to be as tall as the sky. The streets are empty of people, filled with cars, just as they were when we left three months ago.

Our driver gets out first, sliding open the taxi door. He unloads our suitcases, and Justin and I walk over to the metal gate, looking into the parking lot.

I wonder if Johnny and Christian are still here, I say.

You can tell nothing's changed, my brother says. He's right. Even Maman acts as if nothing happened, as if we never left. She doesn't talk about it or ask questions, so I try and be like her, pretending everything is fine. I try to listen to Shawn as he keeps reminding me it was only a few months we were gone, to stop making it into this big deal.

We walk through the building's parking lot. I wave at one of our neighbors, a mom and her two sons. She's carrying groceries, shouting at her kids to help.

I tilt my face up to the sky and close my eyes, telling myself that it's real. We're back, Baba isn't here and he won't be able to take us away again.

When we're inside our building Shawn says, Look around, we're *home*.

To show Shawn just how dramatic I can be I drop my suitcase and lower myself to my knees and kiss the hallway's dirty carpet.

Home sweet home. I smile up at my brothers, at Maman, who's laughing. Divooneh shodeh, she says to Justin and Shawn.

If you had to sleep in Haji Agha's house, I tell Maman, it'd make you crazy, too.

She isn't listening, Shawn says to me.

Yeah, I say, no shit.

III

American Boys

t's time for a change, says Johnny.

After so many scraped elbows and busted knees playing football on the hot gooey gravel of the parking lot, Johnny says we've got to try someplace else. We've got to make the most of the days left before school starts back up.

There's nowhere else, Shawn says. It's either this or the court at the church.

We can always go swimming, Justin says.

Nope, Shawn quickly says back. He still hasn't gotten over the last time we were in the community pool. Some kid took a dump in the water but none of us noticed until tiny chunks were floating around. Shawn started shouting his fucking head off when he realized the dead brown bug beside him wasn't a bug. Johnny and I couldn't stop laughing for the rest of the afternoon, and we always laugh some more each time we remember it.

Johnny says again, It's time for a change.

During the Valley's blazing summer, our moms are always working or too tired to take us to the beach or the movies or even the mall, where at least we'd be able to walk around in the air-conditioning. The boredom gets so bad sometimes I take three showers during the day, just for something to do.

The parking lot behind our building is everything for us. The gap between the dumpsters, where nobody bothers to check because of how bad it smells, is where we go to find cigarette butts with just enough tobacco to light up. And the covered parking spaces to the left, like mini garages there for us to duck into, escaping the hundred-degree heat, stashing empty beer bottles that we find littered on the ground. At night, we fling them at passing cars on Sherman Way, for the sizzle of crashing glass, the high we get as soon as we hear screeching brakes, pounding footsteps as we're being chased, cursed at, adrenaline chomping through our bodies.

Once the sun goes down the three of us, Johnny, Justin and me, sneak into the private school in the next neighborhood over, West Hills. Shawn is off doing his own thing, said he'd rather hoop.

Johnny does it first. Leaps over the chain-link fence in one clean motion. Me and Justin follow behind him, taking our time. We scope out the school, one more fence to climb and now we're sprinting toward a big grassy field, a field we have all to ourselves. We peel off our T-shirts, our warm bodies drinking in the mist from the sprinklers.

Told you this would be a good idea, Johnny shouts over.

Justin walks up to one of the sprinkler heads, stands real close. Like he's in a trance of his own. He keeps his arms raised in the air, his face has a grin, eyes closed. When the sprinkler catches him, the smack of water pounding into my brother's chest becomes the loudest part of the night. It scares me a little, watching his body get hit like this.

I have a feeling he's going to start coming here on his own, I tell Johnny.

Good for him, he tells me. Better than being in the hot-ass parking lot.

anging out with the older boys on a school night, on the lawn in front of our building, I watch as they toss their jokes back and forth, listening as they share their stories and a cigarette, too.

Christian's homies from school ask Johnny to tell it again. They say they saw him sneaking behind the gym last spring with the girl from second period who was crushing on him.

Voices bang into one another as the older boys shout to be the loudest, boldest, but it's Christian's that breaks through the rest. The group hush themselves so they can hear what he has to say. It doesn't matter that Johnny hasn't finished his own story, they already know Christian's is going to be the best. So the group moves on and Johnny doesn't seem to mind. He would rather listen than have to make something up about how far he took things with a girl he barely knows.

Justin, too, who looks bored, leaves to go back inside while Shawn and me wait for Christian to finish, badly wanting to hear the rest of his story.

Now everyone's leaning in, our spines hunched forward, laying our palms into Christian's, because right there on his shorts we see it. The drops that fell from his girlfriend's mouth, forming a white crusted splotch he uses as proof.

Sucking down another drag, Christian's dark brown eyes light up like the red glowing at the end of his cigarette as he pulls in the smoke, and then I feel the group's attention on me. His voice is again getting big, saying that by the time he was my age, he had already gotten head. Keep being a little bitch, he says, and you'll stay a virgin for the rest of your life. Ha ha ha, the group goes, Christian hushing them, saying that the next time I see Crystal, I better make a move. What's so hard about trying? he asks.

I wait for Shawn to jump in, to fill in my quiet with a story of his own, to keep me from looking so dumb in front of the group, like a scared little boy. No matter how badly I want it, my voice won't light up like theirs. My stomach just gets tight, tighter. And now Christian's saying Crystal's name over and again, his hand cupped over his shorts, the group laughing and pointing while he makes his dick twitch and move on its own as though it has a separate pulse. And as he goes on and on we do, too, smiling, pretending, nodding our heads and laughing along, ha ha ha.

Shawn goes, So are you coming or not?

I'm on the sofa and he's standing above me, holding his basketball down to my face, close enough for me to see that his Spalding's covered in dirt, why his baggy T-shirts are always getting dirty.

Go without me, I say, still only halfway awake.

That's why you'll always suck, he says, stuffing his ball into his bag.

If you change your mind you know where to find me, he says, leaving the apartment and slamming the door shut.

I close my eyes and try to fall back asleep.

When next summer comes, time to try out for freshman basketball, if I don't make the team I know what Shawn's going to say. That it's because I was being lazy, didn't practice enough.

This early in the school year and already I'm falling behind in my classes. Several of my teachers are worried I won't pass. I've tried to do better. But each time I sit at the kitchen table to do my algebra homework, or study for a U.S. history test, my mind quickly loses focus.

Already in my shorts and a T-shirt, I go into our room to grab my shoes, then two water bottles from the counter before sprinting outside to catch up with Shawn.

When I make it out onto the street he's waiting for me at the corner, dribbling between his legs. He knew I'd come.

Shawn starts toward the court, one foot in front of the other, my brother doesn't miss a single bounce, the ball sweeping through his legs.

It's his favorite challenge, where if he loses his handle on the ball, he has to start all over and walk back to our apartment, then do it again. It's how you get better, Shawn says.

Three blocks away from the court his rhythm breaks, the ball colliding with his left ankle and right away Shawn leaps from the sidewalk onto the street, chasing down the ball. A car slams on its brakes, and a man with a black beard lunges out, yelling, Kid, are you fucking crazy? The ball gets hit by a van in the opposite lane, then another as it ricochets down Sherman Way.

Shawn darts through the intersection, more cars honking, tires screeching. I look away. No wonder he's so much better than I am. I start to laugh. He'd literally die for basketball.

Shawn walks back onto the sidewalk, winded and sweating, his Spalding clutched to his body. What are you looking at? he says to me. Let's start over.

You know you don't have to take basketball so seriously, I tell him. It's not like it actually matters.

Says *who*? He turns to me, now close to my face. My lazy-ass little brother?

I roll my eyes and consider going back inside but I know that would just prove Shawn's point.

Heading toward Topanga, I follow behind, watching my brother swing the Spalding through his legs, a new rhythm this time with the bounce of the ball harder, faster, beating

into the concrete. As soon as we make it to the court Shawn
takes off his T-shirt and grabs his Jordan jersey from his bag,
the same jersey he wore on the plane coming home from Iran.

Next to an empty church, and surrounded by apartment
buildings, the court isn't really a court but an abandoned
parking lot with a hoop, and Shawn's made it his own. Satur-
days and Sundays he leaves the apartment early in the morning and doesn't get home until after dark. He's even made
friends with some of the other guys who've seen him playing.
When it gets cool enough in the evenings, they run pick-up
games where Shawn gets to use the moves he's practiced
over and over.

The ball falls into my palms from the net. There's no need
for Shawn to chase after his rebounds—he won't miss a shot.

Just make sure you keep giving me my change, he says,
tucking his Jordan jersey deeper into his shorts.

I didn't come here to watch you shoot, I tell him. Let's go
one-on-one already.

Another swish, I pass him his change. What's the point?
he asks.

Check-up, I tell him. And this time don't talk so much
shit, I say. Let's just play.

He exaggerates a sigh, smirking. Don't say I didn't warn
you.

Up to eleven, all ones. Be sure to pay attention, he says,
'cause it's going to go fast.

As he bumps his body into mine, I drive my forearm into
the bottom of his back. I try and keep him out of the key.

It always gets me by surprise how much stronger he is than
me, proving again that just because I'm taller doesn't mean

my body will keep up with his. It can't, never does, and even the older guys who come at night after work to run pickup games—they used to bully Shawn because of his height but not anymore, not after last time when he outscored everyone. And maybe that's why he's always practicing so hard. To make up for the height he doesn't have, barely five foot five.

He pivots on his heels, dribbling with his right hand as he drives his left elbow into the side of my gut, moving toward the hoop for an easy layup, sticking out his tongue in the air just like MJ does.

One–zero.

He drains a jump shot from the top of the key, then another.

Told you, he says as he bounces the ball. Can't stop me.

Shut up and just play, I yell, but I shouldn't have. Because now he knows he's getting in my head.

Keep spending your weekends on the couch. He smirks, driving his shoulder into my chest, then fading away. The ball kisses off the backboard, falls through the net.

Four–zero.

It's too easy, he says, jogging to half court. Gonna suck riding the bench all season next year because you don't practice.

After I check-up, he puts the ball to the pavement, which is when I reach for the steal, the top of his head colliding into my lip.

He doesn't stop, drives to the rim for an uncontested layup.

I can taste metal, my eyes well up with tears and he isn't

slowing down. I hold on to the ball, bent over, wiping the blood from my mouth.

Check-up, he says.

I bounce the ball over to him and again he beats me to the rim but this time when we both leap into the air, I drive my elbow straight into the bridge of his nose. His shot rolls off the rim, I grab the rebound.

I pause, waiting for him to call foul, he doesn't.

Racing to the three-point line I have the ball for the first time, and he's right there trailing behind me, shuffling his feet, digging low into his stance. He shoves his forearm into my back, I try and keep my footing as I circle around on my heels, using the same move he used on me, throwing up a jump shot that doesn't even reach the rim. The ball lands out-of-bounds, his possession.

Shawn watches as the ball rolls toward the gate. There's a thin trickle of blood running from his nose, he wipes it on his jersey.

You're the one who airballed, he says. Go fetch, little boy.

Back at the top of the key I shove the ball into his chest. Check.

Still five—oh, he says, wiping the sweat from his forehead. And quit hacking, not gonna say it again.

He starts by backing me into the paint. I keep my forearm against his lower back and shove my right knee into his bottom. I reach around his body and try to steal the ball.

As he dribbles he uses his free hand to swipe at my arm, to keep me from reaching. But I don't stop fouling him, and this time he elbows me straight in the gut to send a message.

I shove him as hard as I can and he falls to the ground, his stomach landing right on top of the ball.

He's back up within a second lunging toward me and he tackles me to the ground. I hear the back of my head slam against the concrete, and now he's on top of my body burying both of his knees into my chest. He jams down my wrists while I try and break free, using all the strength I have to push his body off mine. I spit up at his face and he keeps yelling at me, telling me to calm the fuck down, slamming my wrists again and again. Then he hawks up a loogie of his own, a green-beaded string of spit swinging down from his mouth, swaying while it hangs inches from my lips. He slurps it back up.

Seriously calm the fuck down, he says. He's looking straight into my eyes, digging his knees farther and farther until it feels like he's going to crack my chest.

For a moment I stop and stay still.

Are you done? he asks.

He begins to ease his grip but now I have just enough space to lift my head, snapping down and biting and digging my teeth into his thigh. He's shouting as loud as his lungs will let him, telling me I'm a fucking animal even though it's him who's acting like one, shrieking and crying. He spits his loogie at me, which lands on the side of my neck, but I've clicked my jaw shut and I won't let go. I don't release until I begin to taste his skin on my tongue, until I see tears falling from Shawn's eyes and I realize I'm hurting him more than I wanted to. I let go, turning my body over with my cheek on the asphalt, panting.

We lie here together, our limbs on the concrete underneath the hoop, Shawn's eyes looking up and through the rim's gray net. I use my shirt to wipe off his spit from my neck, where I can still feel the warm shine of his saliva, like a stamp, stuck to my skin.

Shawn?

After a few moments, nothing.

Shawn.

Yeah? He keeps his voice low.

I lift my back from the ground, sitting up, and feel my heart pounding.

In Iran, I ask, with Baba—Why didn't you make him stop?

My brother sighs big before standing up, and for a second I think he's going to start again, pounding my wrists into the concrete. But he walks over to pick up the ball, clutching onto it. He looks around us, at the abandoned lot that's become his escape, surrounded by flowering red trees that a swarm of bees cling to, glowing in the sunshine.

You don't realize how fucking lucky we were to come back. And not only that, Shawn says, but that Baba stayed in Iran. We get to do whatever we want. He quietly smiles. *Right?* So how about you spend more time thinking about what's in front of us now, rather than some shit that happened over three years ago.

Looking up at my brother, I can tell he's followed his own advice. We haven't spoken to Baba since coming back, and since then Shawn's been making up his own rules as he goes. I can tell he likes who he's becoming, too, confident in this image he's made of himself. Shawn keeps his chin held up, doesn't mumble his sentences the way he used to when Baba lived with us. With his new tapered haircut with sharply lined edges, a trimmed goatee and mustache, Shawn's become handsome as fuck, his light brown eyes excited about the future he sees for himself, whatever that may be.

Back up on my feet, he tells me to check-up, that we still need to finish our game of one-on-one. And as he bumps his shoulder hard into my chest, again using his strength to do whatever he pleases on the court, he tells me I'm gonna have to learn to toughen up, that he's tired of his little brother getting called a bitch whenever we're with our friends and having to watch as I do nothing about it.

t's too hot to be inside, and we're too lazy to move so Johnny and me sit outside in the shade, leaning back and cracking up, doing nothing at all. Still, unlike in class where time feels stuck—with Johnny it goes by so fast. Before we know it the day is over, the sun long gone and we still haven't eaten.

So we go searching for loose change in the cushions of his mom's sofa, coming up with just enough to get ourselves an order of KFC's best new thing. One side of barbecue sauce, one ranch, passing between us the tiny paper box of popcorn chicken—taking our time, savoring each bite.

But tonight after we eat, instead of going inside I tell Johnny we should walk over to the Wash. It's been years since we've gone back.

Two days straight and there's been all this rain, so while it's still full, I tell him, I want to sit by the river.

He knows I don't own a jacket, never have, and he pretends he doesn't have one either. Just in our T-shirts and jeans and we walk to Bassett Street, a few blocks down, then crawl underneath the fence.

We sit together on the cracked concrete slope of the L.A. River, sitting alone with the moon as it lights up the stream below us, the water dark green, almost black, the highest and deepest I've ever seen it. High enough for us to dive in head-first, if we wanted to.

Johnny's sitting close enough so that our shoulders are touching, far enough for there to be enough space so it can happen. All it'd take is for me to tilt my face toward his, tilt it just the tiniest bit—he's older and he knows how this is supposed to go. But I don't, instead just imagining how it would feel, the hairs above his lip prickling against mine, his hot breath.

We watch the dark water of the river, Johnny leaning his weight into mine—his body warm, my body shivering—and even with the voice in my head shouting so loud for his lips, then louder as I lose the moment, it doesn't change the fact that I can't move. As if I'm not in my own body but stuck somewhere other than here.

Until finally he peels his shoulder off mine and stands up, our chance to be together gone.

We better head back, he says, stay any longer and we'll probably get a cold.

When Johnny gets to the other side of the fence, I'm still sitting on the slope by the water. I want to ask him for another chance to try.

I tell him I don't want to go home, and he nods.

Peace out, then, he says. I'll see you tomorrow for Thanksgiving.

Slowly I step down the slope to the river's edge, staring into the water and wanting to jump in, to drown this body that wouldn't let me kiss Johnny. It was as if God had set it up just for us, the moon and its shimmering white light, the rain we so rarely get in the Valley, and Johnny's warm arm against mine. All I had to do was tilt my face the tiniest bit, but even that I couldn't do.

By now I know not to ask Maman if she'll be home. She'll be working, even tonight, even though we don't have any plans, and weren't invited to Christian's New Year's party.

The hospital pays time and a half, she says, putting on her lipstick as she gets ready, spraying on her perfume for the long night ahead.

There's bademjan and rice in the fridge, Maman says. Just heat it in the microwave for a few minutes.

But that food's disgusting, Justin tells her. Can you leave some money for food?

You know what she's going to say, Shawn says. *She cooked the eggplant for a reason.*

Exactly, Maman's face says. She reminds us to lock the door behind her.

When Shawn gets up from the sofa I ask him if I can change the channel, he says he doesn't care. I turn it to 52, MTV, watching what looks like a million people huddled in the cold, dressed in gloves and beanies and scarves, things we don't own.

You couldn't pay me to stand in the fucking cold like that, my brother says as he puts on his shoes, then reaches for his basketball.

C'mon, he tells me. Get up and let's go to the court.

Right now? The lights aren't going to be on.

So what, he says. Better than being here.

Shawn knows not to bother asking Justin, who'd rather spend the night by himself reading in our room. When I don't say anything Shawn picks up his bag and puts in his jersey, leaving Justin and me alone.

Justin goes into the kitchen, reaches into the cabinet where Shawn hides his cereal (our brother won't admit it but he's addicted to Fruity Pebbles), pours himself a bowl and sets it down on the coffee table, then goes back to pour me one, too. We're out of milk, so he uses water instead.

We finish the box, not caring about what Shawn will do when he finds out. And after Justin rinses out our bowls in the sink, he tells me I should spend less time watching TV. I tell him he should join me on the sofa for the countdown, he's going to miss the ball drop.

Doesn't really mean anything, he says, just another day.

He turns to the middle of his book, a pen in his hand as he reads, the other running over the thick hooped earring, which he put in himself, using Maman's sewing needle to pierce his right earlobe last month.

Did you already finish the last one you were reading? I ask him.

Yesterday, he tells me, looking up from the table. Started this one right away, he says, holding up the book for me to see, telling me he found it in the closet wedged between Maman's old nursing textbooks, and that when he asked where it came from she said she had to read it for one of her college electives, but that she never did. She just had her classmate summarize it for her. My brother laughs.

I walk over from the sofa and he hands me the book, tucking his pen inside to make sure I don't lose his spot on the page. It's a slim novel, can't be more than 150 pages, which Justin says he'll probably finish by the morning.

The title *Siddhartha* is in bold white letters at the top of the front cover, over a dark blue background, a bronze statue of him sitting with his legs crossed, one palm resting open on his lap.

I'm only halfway through, Justin tells me, but so far it's become my new favorite book.

The cover's beautiful, I tell him.

You should read it when I'm done, he says.

It'd probably put me to sleep.

Or it would teach you something important, my brother says.

Like flunking out of high school?

Ever since the end of last semester, Justin stopped showing up to his classes. Justin, who used to be the smartest of the three of us, and the hardest working.

He chuckles, shaking his head. You love being a smart-ass, don't you?

Why should I bother, he then says, to sit around for six hours a day at a school that doesn't give a shit about me?

Everything I need is right here, Justin tells me, taking *Siddhartha* from my hand. He goes back to reading.

So now what, I ask him, you're just going to let yourself become one of those losers who drops out?

Almost whispering, as if he's talking to himself, he says, It's called a GED, you dumbass. Then he shuts his book, looking up at me. Why don't you just mind your own fucking business and go back to the sofa, he tells me, pointing to the TV. Wouldn't want you to miss your precious countdown.

Later I see Johnny sitting on the staircase, smoking, his back toward me. I can recognize him even from this end of the path. I walk toward him, holding out my hand to ask for a drag. Pulling the smoke down to my lungs, I look straight into Johnny's face, his hazel eyes that he says came from his mom's side of the family, the Puerto Rican side, which for Johnny is the only family he gets to have—his dad lives in Texas and barely comes around. But tonight he's got on the birthday gift his dad sent three years ago when Johnny turned thirteen, the only birthday gift he's ever gotten from him, a vintage Houston Astros jersey, yellow and red with a big star underneath his chest. Johnny wears it tucked into his dark blue jeans with a silver chain around his neck. He swears that in a different life he would've been the greatest shortstop to ever live, and as he sprawls across the staircase I believe him. His chest and shoulders look fit, strong. But it's his long and tan arms that are my favorite, how the veins in his lean muscles show without him having to flex, which started appearing last summer, after his growth spurt got him up to five-ten. He's the tallest in our group. And now he likes to keep his dark hair buzzed, faded, to look less like a boy and more like a man, he says, his chin and upper lip peppered with tiny bits of facial hair, brown skin that glistens.

Everyone go home? I ask him.

Nah, Johnny says. They knocked out at Christian's. It's like they've never had alcohol before. He laughs, lighting another cigarette.

Wish I could have been there, I tell him.

You know how he is. Says he doesn't want little kids hanging around, acts as if we're grown just because we like to get fucked up.

Yeah, I say, whatever.

I sit down on the step below him, my back against the railing, letting the rain fall on my shoulders.

Feels good, Johnny says, doesn't it?

The sky again opening for us, I reach back and stick out my tongue to catch the drops of rain.

But same here, he tells me.

I sit up straight, wiping the rain from my face.

It would've been better with you there, Johnny says, now reaching back with his mouth, too, keeping it open for the rain.

Maman waits until the very last moment possible, right as she pulls beside the curb outside of my school, to tell me she won't be able to stay for my graduation. She's in her hospital scrubs, fumbling over her words as she says she tried but wasn't able to get her shift covered in time, that they're making her go.

On my way out of the car she tells me how handsome I look, me in my brown tie and fresh white button-up with Shawn's dark blue slacks from when he graduated three years ago. Make sure you ask your friends' parents to take pictures of you, she says, when you're up there on the stage.

Onstage I stand with my eighth-grade diploma, shaking the principal's hand, smiling for no one. A sea of parents and younger siblings, grandparents driven into town for this special day are squinting and sweating beneath the white sun on the school's big lawn, cameras around their necks.

I pretend they're there for me. Pretend I don't care that Maman is missing from the crowd. But more than Baba or Shawn or Justin or even Johnny, I want Maman to watch me graduate from eighth grade—Maman, who understands how hard it is to finish school. There were so many moments when I didn't think I'd be allowed to. Cheating on my assignments and stealing from the internet, talking back in class and getting sent out, worst of all in my final month of middle school being caught by my science teacher when I turned in Justin's lab notebook from the prior year. I scratched out his name and handed it in as if my teacher wouldn't notice. As if I had kept up throughout the semester and took notes, like we were instructed to, on the lab experiments conducted in class. When I was called into the main office after my teacher reported what I had done, my counselor held the black composition notebook in her hand, threatening to expel me for defiance and plagiarism. I sat in the chair, shivering from the air conditioner blasting straight down on me, wondering how my counselor could sit in the cold all day. I did my best not to show any emotion, a smirk on my face instead. I didn't want her to know I felt bad for what I did. I could tell she hated me. She had a long tense face, stuck and cold. I stared at the burn marks on the right side of her chin, trailing down her neck, I imagined what it was that happened, how much of her body had been burned, and if it was the reason she was now so harsh, why she liked being cold. She let me know my behavior would land me in prison one day, and that if it was up to her, she said, I'd never be allowed back to the school.

I watch my classmates being hugged and praised, parents teary-eyed and proud, my counselor congratulating the top students, draping them with medals of excellence and certificates for three years of perfect attendance. When my turn comes and I walk across the stage I want to thank her for giving me another chance, to let her know I'm sorry and how much it means to me that I still get to graduate, but my counselor won't look at me.

I don't stay for the rest of the ceremony, don't feel like I deserve to. I walk home by myself, tossing my diploma into the trash. I didn't really earn it so why should I keep it, and why should Maman get to see it when she wasn't even there.

The next morning when Maman gets home from work, she comes into our room to wake me up, running the back of her hand along my cheek, waiting for me to open my eyes. She places four tickets onto my lap. For years me and my brothers have been asking Maman to take us to Six Flags. Your graduation present, Maman says, smiling big.

It's Sunday when we go and Maman's up before the three of us, packing our lunches for the day. Pita bread stuffed with Persian mortadella, slices of tomato and pickles and mayonnaise—Mary's Famous Sandwich, Shawn likes to call it. I'm in charge of helping her navigate, using the sheet of paper she scribbled directions onto. It's an hour drive, at least, to Valencia, and usually Maman avoids freeways because they make her anxious, but for today she makes an exception.

We take the 118 Freeway across to the 5 and as we approach our exit, there in the distance we see it. We stare in awe at Colossus's towering drop, its white wooden tracks glowing underneath the sun, suspended in the sky as if it's a staircase descending from the clouds.

No fucking way I'm getting on that, Justin points.

Ehh, Maman shouts, her Persian version of scolding us for cursing, but of course that doesn't stop us.

I knew it, Shawn says. Too late to pussy out now, he tells Justin as we pull in the parking lot. We're already here.

Just wait, Justin tells him, I won't be the one who shits all over himself, which makes us laugh, Maman included, because what Justin's saying is true. Out of the three of us Shawn's got the weakest stomach, even if he refuses to admit it. He eats whatever he wants and does whatever he feels like doing, and if he pukes or has diarrhea, which happens often, whatever.

Everyone shits, he's always saying, mine's just a little waterier.

So of course it ends up being Shawn and me who ride Colossus, three times straight while Justin goes to the arcade using the quarters Maman usually reserves for laundry.

Afterward, we convince Maman to ride with us, but we have to pick a different roller coaster. She refuses to get on Colossus.

We choose Revolution, it has only one loop without any big drops and there isn't even a line to get on, which goes to show you just how lame the roller coaster is, we tell Maman, half lying and half not.

Me and Shawn laugh so hard on the ride, tricking Maman into riding a roller coaster knowing she's terrified of heights. The way the other parents are shrieking as us kids shoot our arms straight up, I expect Maman to be screaming, too, but she keeps her eyes shut the entire time, not making a single sound.

Shawn even buys the picture that was captured of us, where Maman looks like a ghost, the color from her face gone, with me and Shawn nearly falling out of our seats, my face flushed and our cheeks blown out.

I need to sit, Maman says as we're walking down the ramp to exit the ride, and Shawn races to the arcade to join Justin, saying he doesn't want to waste any time.

Maman finds an empty bench and as soon as we sit she starts to massage the back of her neck, saying she isn't feeling well, not at all. She's having a hard time breathing and she takes out an inhaler from her purse, which I've never seen her use before. There's nothing for me to do to make it better. I hate seeing Maman like this, afraid.

I'm sorry we lied, Maman. But on the ride you weren't even scared.

How do you know that, she snaps back, still trying to loosen the muscles in her neck.

You didn't make a sound the entire time, I tell her. Didn't you hear the other adults yelling and screaming? I ask as she takes out our lunch from her bag, the sandwiches wrapped in plastic, bread that's soaked in pink-red juice from the crushed tomatoes. When she hands one to me I press through it with my fingers, feeling for the parts that aren't soggy, there are none. I try my best not to show how gross the sandwich feels, keeping it on my lap without looking down at it.

Maman takes the sandwich from me, unwrapping it, and she goes for the first bite of the soggy bread as one of the park's Looney Tunes characters leaps out in front of us. Maman, with a mouthful of tomato and mortadella and pickles, tells them off. Boro gomsho, she shouts at Bugs Bunny, who's dancing and singing, reaching over and grabbing Maman by the arm, calling her over to join the crowd, to take pictures. Really, I yell at Bugs, she's not feeling well. The person in the costume offers us their fake carrot and then moonwalks away, back to the dancing crowd.

Maman rips off tiny pieces of soggy bread for the birds now gathering around us at our feet.

She shakes her head. When I was little, younger than you are now, I had a fever that got so bad at night I was having hallucinations. Four days straight it went on, Maman says, and when Baba-jan came into my room I couldn't talk. I was sweating and sweating, my body had no water left. When he took my temperature it read 104.

Can you believe that? she asks me.

104, I repeat, shaking my head and keeping myself from asking more, staying out of Maman's way.

Khoda biamorzesh, she says, taking another bite. Baba-jan didn't own a car, so to get to the hospital I rode on the back of his bicycle. And when we got there, Maman says, starting from the middle of a story she's never told me before, the doctor asked Baba-jan why didn't he bring me sooner. Any longer, the doctor said to him, and your daughter would be dead.

Do you know why I remembered that? Maman asks me.

I shake my head.

Baba-jan replied with the same thing you just said, Maman tells me. That I didn't make a single sound.

She stares down at her sandwich, considering another bite before turning to me. There's a shine in both of her eyes, and I wonder if they're tears wanting to come up, or just the way Maman's eyes always look. That doesn't mean I wasn't in pain, she tells me.

Then how come you didn't ask for help, I say to her.

With the small smile on her face, it's as if Maman's talking about someone else's life, remembering a time that to her doesn't feel real.

At home and at masjid and in school, Maman tells me, the

best thing for me was to stay quiet. And it worked, because look where I am now. I have my own life, Maman says, as she wipes the crumbs from her lap.

She wraps the sandwich back in its plastic. You don't look very hungry, she tells me. How do you know that, I quickly say before we stand to go, pretending to mock her and snapping back the way she did earlier, hoping it'll make Maman laugh, will take her away from the past. I want Maman to know she doesn't have to be quiet anymore, that it'd be better. That way I'd get to know who she actually is. She'd get to know me, too. But she repeats it again, how for her being quiet has worked, even at the hospital, nobody bothers her because she keeps to herself.

Sheytoon, she calls me as I keep teasing her. Maman grabs at my ear, lightly twisting it, and it's the first time in a while she brings my face to hers, giving me a kiss on the forehead— her favorite troublemaker, Maman calls me.

Bringing the leftovers from the Fourth of July, Christian comes by our apartment with a box of fireworks.

Ours to use? Justin asks.

Christian grins. Damn right.

Let's go out to the parking lot, then, I tell them.

First grab a lighter, Christian says. Mine's a piece of shit, he tells us, tossing it aside.

Doesn't Maman keep one in the kitchen? I ask Justin.

He goes to look, opening drawers and digging through papers and bills.

I can't find the lighter, Justin shouts. And there aren't any matches, either.

He's back at the door holding a purple stick of incense instead.

Christian laughs. What are we supposed to do with that?

I can light it using the stove, my brother tells him, and we can bring it outside to use for the fireworks.

It won't work, Christian says.

Let's at least try, my brother tells him.

Justin goes back to the kitchen, with Christian and me following behind.

Do it here so we don't waste time, Christian says. If it lights, I'll put it out with my fingers, he shows us, pinching the fuse between his thumb and middle finger. But I'm telling

you, he says. It's not going to work. You can't light a firework with fucking incense.

Justin turns on the stove, lighting the stick, its rich sweet
smell filling our apartment. Bring it here, he tells Christian,
his eyes growing bigger.

Justin holds the stick's glowing red nub against the tip of
the fuse.

Told you, Christian says, it was a stupid—

There are sparks flying through the kitchen and then a
chorus of *Oh shit* as Justin pinches at the fuse while Christian
just keeps staring. Justin is trying to put it out only it won't
work. He's trying to stop the fuse even though moments ago
Christian said he'd be the one to do it, and the sparks keep
going and my brother keeps yelling, Why won't it stop? And
now Christian's backing away from the fuse that's disappearing right between my brother's fingers.

Justin turns to me, shoves me and tells me to hide because
it's about to blow and that's when I dive behind Maman's
sofa where Christian is already crouching, the two of us
ducking our heads as if it were an earthquake drill at school,
drop cover hold, when I hear the explosion and I peek over
the couch and what I find is more color than I've ever seen
before, flying from Justin's palm.

He tosses the firework into the sink but it's too late because the curtains by our dining table catch fire and the smoke
alarms scream at us.

Buckets, Christian yells once the firework finally goes out.
Where do you guys keep buckets?

Justin yanks open the oven where Maman keeps her pots,

he grabs as many as he can hold and rushes to the bathroom tub to fill them.

When he returns he throws the water onto every small fire that's started in our apartment, smoke everywhere, alarms still blaring, and any second now I know the police will be here and we'll be arrested for doing something so dumb, so illegal.

But they don't, not the police or the fire department, not even our neighbors come knocking on our door.

Nobody asks where Maman is, why we decided to light fireworks inside. Just us, the three of us sitting on the charred carpet with craters scattered all throughout the floor, pretending that we weren't scared, that we knew exactly what was going to happen, that we had it all under control. Of course that's how we wanted it, to watch it explode inside, more color than we've ever seen.

You should have been there, I tell Maman.

It's been a week and she's finally looking me in the eye again after what happened with the fireworks. The holes we burnt into the carpet, it's a miracle that none of the sparks landed on Maman's Persian rug.

Maman's on the sofa, her checkbook open across her lap, looking through her mail, tearing open envelopes and paying bills. I squeeze my body next to hers. Everyone lost their minds, I tell Maman. Shawn beat an *all-American*. The best player in all of California.

Maman's glancing over her blue checkbook, a calculator in one hand and a pencil in the other, her thick black reading glasses on.

At first I couldn't watch, I tell her, I thought he'd get embarrassed to the point where he wouldn't ever again go back to the court. I even prayed, I tell Maman, who briefly looks up, tearing out a check and placing it into an envelope, then licking it sealed.

I stand up, smiling, remembering the look on Malcolm's face. By the end, I tell Maman, it was Trevor's little brother who couldn't watch.

It was magic, like nothing I've ever seen. And since he didn't miss a single shot, not fucking once, Trevor never even *touched* the ball.

Maman, I shout, jolting her so that I get her attention, the calculator dropping from her palm. I reach down to pick it up as Maman begins to pack her things.

Shawn was better than I've ever seen him, I continue, than he'll ever be. It was like he transformed into an NBA player for those five plays.

The older guys invited him out to lunch afterward, I tell Maman. That's who he's been hanging out with ever since. Shawn has a crew of his own now.

Baseh digeh, she says. I understand. She walks over to the kitchen, checking on the rice and chicken she's making before she leaves, then asks me to turn off the stove in five minutes, she's going to take a shower before work.

Watching Shawn with my mouth hung open and eyes glued to his every bounce, I was so happy in that moment to be Shawn's youngest brother. And I knew if he were there, Baba would've been impressed, too.

To our dad basketball was something so foreign and pointless. Once, tossing the basketball into my brother's hands, he asked Shawn, as a joke, if he thought he'd become as good as Kareem Abdul-Jabbar, to prove he at least knew of *one* professional player, knowing Shawn would never be as tall, not even close.

It took my brother more than five years to answer Baba's question, but last week, he did. Using the skyhook Kareem used to win five championships for L.A., Shawn became just as righteous on the court. It was my first time seeing him like that. Silent and strong and so focused, I couldn't recognize my brother from before.

My feet reach the bottom and I start to walk toward Johnny, my body moving slowly, wading in the water. He's sitting by the silver rail that drops into the pool, his knees tucked into his chest, and as I get closer he slides over, making room for me on the steps. The heavy swoosh of the water pushes up his trunks, showing the beginning of his thighs where his skin is a little lighter. Over there in the deep end, Christian and Shawn are jumping in and climbing back out, using the smack of their bodies to churn out waves. The water laps onto our stomachs. I watch as the thick black hairs on Johnny's shins brush underneath, wishing that one day my legs would look like his.

With the sun almost gone now the chill of dusk settles into our skin, our bodies rattling and legs drifting, knees gently rocking and then touching where Johnny keeps them pressed against mine, quiet. Strings like red confetti are scattered in the white of his eyes—I can feel their sting in my own. You shouldn't open them under water, I say. He lifts his hand and scratches and rubs at his eyelids, as if that'll make the red go away.

Let's get out, I tell him. It's getting cold. Johnny moves the back of his body up the steps and I do the same, both of us leaning with our palms on the concrete edge. I let my hands flatten into the chilled puddles of water, my fingers stretching and inching toward his.

We finally bought a PlayStation, I tell Johnny. I say that he should come over.

He chuckles. To play video games?

Plus, I tell him, picking at the loose fabric on my shorts, my mom isn't home.

As he stands up I do the same, and we don't dry ourselves because we didn't bring towels. We never do. Shawn and Christian are watching as we leave through the pool's rusted pink gate. Come over after you guys are done, Johnny shouts.

We'll be chillin here, Christian says.

Shawn nods his head at me, smiles as he lands another cannonball into the pool, the biggest splash he's made yet so that the water reaches us through the gate. Johnny is laughing. How does your brother get his tiny-ass body to make such a massive splash?

Once we're alone walking toward the apartment, it's hard to know what to say. If Christian were here with us he'd do the talking, would probably even laugh if he saw how quiet I'm being. So I search through my mind looking for a story I can bring back from those nights by the staircase, though wouldn't Johnny know that I'm just stealing lines, pretending they're mine?

I lead us through the same hallway we've wandered through so many times before, and though I know this place and for years it's been home, now it's different and new. The corridors that've always felt too long are shorter, as if I've become bigger, the thin lines of yellow running along the cracked stucco walls feeling sharper against my fingertips.

Once we're inside I show him our PlayStation and put in the one game we own, Need for Speed. I wait for it to load, both of us sitting on my bed, staring at the screen. My legs are shaking. I give Johnny the line I've practiced from before, planning it for an afternoon like this one, after swimming, knowing Maman isn't home, knowing she won't be for a while and that Justin is out with his friends.

Think I'm gonna go take a bath before we start, I tell Johnny. Get this nasty smell of chlorine off me.

I'll be here, he says, without looking up.

In the bathroom I look for something to make bubbles with, reaching over to twist open the faucet. Then I step back and lean against the door, pushing my ear into it listening as Johnny paces around the room.

The faucet droning on and on, I slide down my shorts and I notice myself growing, now hard. I start to touch myself and then there's a loud thump against the door, breaking through the noise of the running water. The thump becomes more, Johnny knocking on the other side.

I put my shorts back on, open the door all the way and he steps in.

Got bored in there, he says, looking down at the tag sticking out from the front of my shorts, smiling. He leaps up and onto the sink, stringing the yo-yo he picked up from my bed.

Haven't messed with one of these in a while, he says. Think I can still Gravity Pull?

Steam crawls up the mirror behind him and I'm glad. I don't want to see the red glow I know my cheeks now have.

The water rises to the brim of the tub, almost overflowing. I shut off the faucet and look into the tub, Johnny's eyes are digging through the back of my shoulders, I can feel them.

It looks like it's blue inside, I tell him. Doesn't it?

Johnny nods. It's 'cause of the old pipes, he tells me. Makes the water blue, but I kinda like it, he says, feels like you're in your own pool.

By the time you're done staring it's gonna get cold, he says, so again I slide off my shorts, turning my back to him. Untangle my ankles, raise my foot over and dip my toes into the tub.

How is it? he asks.

I turn to face him, goosebumps running up my back and arms. Like heaven, I say, slowly lowering my body in as I cup my hands over myself, making sure Johnny can't see that compared to him and the other older boys who are always measuring their dicks talking about how big they are, I know I'm much smaller.

You were right, he tells me, lifting his forearms to his face, smelling his own skin—the chlorine does fucking stink.

I tell him there's room if he wants to join me.

Scoot over then, he says. It's my first time hearing Johnny's voice like this, shaky, nervous.

As he sits on the ledge, he swings around his legs and drops his feet into the water, tucking them beneath me. He leans over and with both of his hands splashes his face, the water dropping over his shoulders and chest.

He notices me growing, getting hard again, we're watching each other now.

Have you done this before? he asks.

I don't answer, for a moment looking away, then back at Johnny's face.

Together we watch the small whirl of water gathering underneath the faucet, being sucked down. When he asks if we should turn the tap back on, with both hands I reach for his waist, peeling off his shorts. There's a chorus of sharp sounds as the drain takes the last of the tub's water, leaving just the two dots on the drain's silver rim, rusted and orange. I dip my head and fill my mouth with Johnny's skin, tasting him, traces of chlorine still lingering from our afternoon, his dick bitter and warm and salty on my tongue, his taste spreading throughout.

I lift up my head wanting to see his eyes, to make sure this is okay for him. More, Johnny whispers, his eyes closed. So good, he tells me as he pushes his body against my mouth where gently I kiss him all over, brushing my lips through the trail of brown hair running down his stomach, kissing the inside of his thighs, my mouth and my tongue moving to his waist, over to his arms.

My fingers around the extra skin of his dick that mine doesn't have, the tip of his penis gleaming with a bright and warm pink. You're so beautiful, I whisper to Johnny, my body beginning to shiver. Let's turn the water back on, I tell him.

Hurry then, he whispers.

I reach over and twist open the faucet, listening as the crash of water fills the quiet in the bathroom. My hot breath is covering him as he clenches his fists and again shuts his eyes, his head swings back as he thrusts himself past the end of my tongue and deeper into my throat. I feel for how far he can go. I keep my eyes open. I move faster, up and down, and his knees start twitching, his breath catching and voice trembling—I'm going to finish, he says, his hand now grabbing and pulling on my hair. Not yet, I whisper, pulling him out and moving away as the warm water rises around us, our pruned toes and fingers softening.

Let's keep going, I say.

What do you mean?

As I turn around the tub overflows, a small flood of water on the bathroom floor reaching for the door. My head underneath the faucet, its waterfall pouring down my neck. Lifting my palms and placing them on each side of the tub I curve my back and lower my head, my bottom facing his chest. For so long I've wanted to feel what it's like to have Johnny inside my body. And this time it's me who gets to choose.

But Johnny doesn't move or say anything. He stays on the edge of the tub, his penis now soft. I thought you've done this before, I say, looking over my shoulder.

Not this, he says as he looks away from me. He steps out of the tub and onto the bathroom floor, his back to me as he puts on his shorts.

Let's go back outside, he tells me.

I let my palms move away from the edge, dunking myself under. *K*, I hear him saying, his voice rippling through the water, but I won't come up. For a moment longer Johnny watches me from the door, until finally he turns to leave. With the faucet's waterfall still crashing into the tub, I close my eyes underneath the blue water.

IV

Our New Millennium

The voice of Bob Costas is booming through our living room six months into the new year, what everyone's been calling the New Millennium. It's a hot and sweaty night, the three of us huddled on Maman's sofa staring at the screen of our blinking TV, Shaq and Kobe together minutes away from bringing home the title, their first ring.

Up until halftime it was just Shawn and me, shouting each time the Pacers got the ball, and it must've been the yelling that got Justin to come join us. He stood by the kitchen counter, waiting, leaning against the wall and eventually Shawn scooted over into the corner of the sofa, nudging me to do the same on the opposite side. Like this we made space for our brother, who squeezed his body between ours, the three of us chanting along, my eyes glued to the Lakers' every move.

And now, the closer it gets to the end the quieter we get. My Kobe jersey is sticking to my skin and looking like his, soaked in sweat as if it were me playing all forty-eight minutes of the championship game. The three of us focus, the heat seeping through our apartment walls, beads of sweat down the sides of our faces.

Hearing someone with a voice so different from ours calling the play-by-play of the biggest game on the biggest stage, Bob Costas's Queens accent makes it feel even more important, special, sitting here with my brothers listening as the cheers from the Staples Center erupt and chime through our living room.

This deep into the fourth quarter, with only three minutes left, Hack-a-Shaq begins. Each time the Lakers get possession, right away the Pacers foul, give Shaq a pair of free throws. Chances are he'll miss.

He steps up to the line and I can't bear looking. It hurts, watching as the Most Dominant Player in the NBA fumbles with the ball, trying to focus his aim. The Spalding that's cupped in Shaq's palm looks like a marble would in mine. Guiding it into the hoop from fifteen feet away feels impossible.

So Shawn becomes my eyes, but he won't tell me if Shaq missed and only when I look again do I realize that he did.

Back to stomping my feet, chanting along with the crowd, the three of us yelling as loud as we can. It's Jalen Rose with the ball, driving to the hole, and he throws up a shot over Shaq's outstretched palm. I hold my breath. The ball is less than an inch away from falling in, before rolling off the lip of the rim.

The Lakers advance the ball up the court and you can see him standing at the wing, Kobe calling for the rock.

Get him the ball, I shout at the TV.

Dump it into Shaq, Shawn yells.

Every fan at Staples can feel it, Kobe's time to shine—twenty-one years old and he's been waiting for this moment his entire life. As a high schooler he studied MJ's every move, practicing and training and working so hard to become a champion, to become the greatest.

One-on-one, Kobe's got his defender isolated at the top

of the key, sizing him up and lulling him to sleep, a quick hesitation before crossing the ball over and then *BAM!* Bob Costas erupts and the three of us do, too, leaping to our feet as Kobe dances back to the bench mouthing to the crowd, I told you, I got *this*.

Lakers up six and it's timeout Pacers.

They're gonna fucking *win*, I shout as the same Taco Bell commercial plays on a loop.

We'll celebrate with chalupas if they do, Shawn says, pointing at the TV.

Justin jets to the fridge and when he returns he's got three Popsicles in his hands. Better than nothing, he says.

The sticky red juice drips into my lap when the Pacers take the final shot, the clock on the bottom right corner of the screen reads *0.00*.

What happens next nobody could have predicted, not Shawn or Justin or me, not Bob Costas and not even Shaq himself.

Kobe leaps into the air and pumps his fist. And as soon as he finds Shaq at center court he lunges into his chest, hanging from the Big Fella's neck as Shaq keeps him clutched in one arm, the other pointing into the air. And that's when I pause. I don't say anything. The smile splashed across Kobe's face is brighter than the arena's lights, than the sparkling confetti falling from the rafters.

The NBA's Greatest Duo, as though they had rehearsed this very move, as if they were made for this moment. Kobe showing the world what it's like to have an older brother you can count on, strong enough to hold you up for the world to see its new champion, even higher than you dreamed of.

Shawn turns to me and Justin, his voice suddenly serious, says that one day we'll get our turn, too. That just like Shaq and Kobe the three of us will make it all the way to the top, our brother promises.

At the end of the night, after feasting on chalupas like Shawn said we would, tossing around on sheets damp from my own sweat—I whisper over to him and ask my brother what it is we have to do, now that we promised one another our lives would feel just as important, as real, as the Lakers'.

Whenever Justin leaves our apartment he goes away for two or three days at a time, comes back home reeking of weed. If Maman happens to catch him on his way in she demands to know where he was and why he was out so late. My brother answers her questions with a shrug and a grin, reminding her that he's almost eighteen.

He never goes without his skateboard, his backpack stuffed with a stick of deodorant, swimming trunks and a change of clothes. Skating all the way to the other side of the Valley, he meets up with friends I've never met, riding buses and trains I've never even heard of. Using the Red Line to get to Hollywood, Justin's discovered more of L.A. all on his own, sneaking into concerts and movies, bars that don't ask him and his friends for ID.

And depending on his mood when he gets home, because with Justin you just never know, sometimes he'll wake me, asking me to join him in the kitchen as he makes his favorite late-night bite, quesadillas stuffed with so much cheese none of it actually melts. That's how I get to hear the stories of where he was, the things he got to see, secret conversations that I promise to keep to myself.

But tonight, as he stumbles into our room from a Fourth of July pool party he's been looking forward to all summer, I hear Justin on my own without him having to shake me awake. He's undressing in the dark, the music playing through his Sony Walkman so loud I can make out every word—"Chop Suey" by System of a Down. Their lead singer is the only dude in rock who looks anything like us, so they've become his favorite band and *Toxicity* the only album he owns, often listening to it on repeat, even this late at night.

He goes out to the kitchen and I get out of bed, hoping it'll be one of those nights he lets me stay with him as he cooks.

He's standing in front of the refrigerator, a container of cheddar cheese in one hand, a bag of tortillas in the other. Staring straight ahead as if he's forgotten where he is, lost in the music blaring through his headphones, even before he says it, I can tell something has happened.

When he notices me standing there, he shouts, I'm in love, his voice too loud in the quiet of the apartment, the middle of the night. Outside even the fireworks have stopped. Our neighbors are asleep and exhausted from celebrating America's independence, a full day of drinking, swimming and eating and vomiting.

Justin's eyes are buzzing, a smile so big on his face that at first I don't recognize him. And as I sit here listening to where he was, what he did and how he spent his Fourth, I know what he's telling me isn't something he's made up, but a kind of love that's real, something that's been happening over the last few months.

He met her downtown, at a table tucked away in L.A.'s Central Library, where Justin's been spending his afternoons, getting there by train. Carrying around a stack of poetry, he tells me, she joined me at my table, the only available chair in the aisle. Thank God for that empty seat, my brother says as he smiles.

That's so romantic it's actually gross, I joke.

Right? He lets himself laugh.

He tells me how whenever he's with her, he feels a kind of happiness he thought he'd never get to have, and unlike the other boys would, my brother doesn't go into the details, nothing about how fine she is, what a bomb-ass body she has. He doesn't tell me about the things they've done with each other in bed. He chooses his words carefully, pausing in between to check on his food, Justin says it's as though he's been looking for her his entire life, nobody else.

Her dad's a vet, he tells me, and he's going to get Justin a job at his clinic in West Hills.

We know where we're going to live, too. Last weekend we went to check it out. Her dad's business partner is renovating their guest house. We'll have a pool and our own backyard to use. Should be ready in a few months for us to move in.

Sounds too good to be true, I want to tell him, but that's just me being jealous of what my brother gets to have, the way he's already imagined their future together, where they'll live as adults, without any rules, the way he wants to.

And how about you, little bro, Justin asks me. Anything new?

Orientation for work takes place a week later in a building that from the street seems abandoned, tucked away in a forgotten lot like so many others in Canoga Park. Beside the building is an office with tons of signs advertising legal services and unemployment insurance and safe-driving classes, not a single person inside of it.

The fourteen of us gather in a small room with long white lights, air-conditioning that keeps us shivering, and right from the start the HR lady dismisses a bunch of the new hires, because of wrist and finger tattoos that can't be hidden or documents that can't be provided.

By the time the orientation starts, there are six of us left.

When I hand her my social security card, for the first time she doesn't look angry. She staples a copy to my employee packet, takes a long look around the room, whispering under her breath that it's refreshing to hire someone who isn't an illegal.

She doesn't mention anything about my age. I lied when I first applied, figured they'd be more likely to hire me if they thought I was eighteen, anything to start making money the way Shawn was, getting to buy new Sean John clothes. He even bought a shitty used car with what he saved up from his job at Champ's, where he's been promoted to assistant manager, working full-time, selling basketball shoes.

When I submit yet another faulty W4 form—crossing out my mistakes as though they'd go undetected—the HR lady has this look on her face that makes me think she's going to hit me. For the remainder of the orientation her cheeks are permanently flushed, making it even harder for me and the five others not to laugh as she scolds me, telling me I get one last chance or I won't be hired if I can't even fill out a form correctly.

Go down the hall and make a right, she says. When you finish the video on sexual harassment, remember to complete the quiz at the end.

Afterward we're taken to the store manager, Daryl, who has an office inside the McDonald's restaurant. He schedules me for three consecutive shifts, starting tomorrow, to shadow and train at all three stations, drive-thru and fryer and front register.

I show up early for my first shift, wanting Daryl to think highly of me. I'm already dressed in my uniform, anything to avoid the dank and dark locker room, where the must of potatoes and sweat is permanently wedged into the tiles of the wall. No, thank you, I told him when he offered me a locker, wiping the oil that had settled on my skin and already seeped into my pores after only a few minutes of touring the back of the kitchen. I made sure not to let Daryl notice how grossed out I was when I saw one of the cooks sliding open a drawer in a rack above the huge iron griddle, where he was storing rows of small cooked patties. Though what did I expect— I guess this is why they call it fast food, patties pulled on the fly, ready to go.

My leather nonslip shoes are freshly polished, and my button-up, which Maman helped me iron, crisp and clean, is tucked into my black pants, which are two sizes too small. With my pants hiked above my ankles, revealing the white cotton socks I wear to my first day, my coworker Brian stands laughing beside me as I clock in for my shift.

Nobody told me I'd have the King of Pop shadowing me, he says, leaning in and slapping me on my back.

Me and the other crew members stay quiet, none of us understanding the joke, and the smirk leaves Brian's face.

When you come back tomorrow, he says, just be sure to wear black socks.

I nod.

Good. He smiles, this time slapping me in the chest. Welcome to Mickey D's, kid.

Standing on my feet for eight hours taking orders at the drive-thru, my legs are beat and my head pounding from the headset's ping chiming in my ear since early in the morning. But I know if I go home now I'll just end up lying down for a nap and regretting it later at night, when I'm unable to sleep, tossing and turning. If nothing else, joining my brother and his friends on the court I'll get in a good workout, sweating away the fryer's thick oil that buried its way into my forehead and cheeks.

When I arrive in the lot behind the church on Topanga, the three of them are finishing up a game of 21, and as I watch it becomes obvious Shawn wasn't exaggerating. Making his defenders stumble and trip over their own heels, when my brother rises into the air for a jumper, the ball splashes through the net as he scores. It's like water, he says. He's the best one on the court, and if Shawn weren't so short maybe he would, actually, have a chance at playing college ball, who knows maybe even play pro overseas.

We run two-on-two for two hours straight, me and Shawn putting his friends to work—pick-and-rolls and give-and-goes, we make sure whenever we have the rock not to stop moving on the court. My brother scores most of our points while I lock up on defense, once even diving onto the pavement for the loose ball, scuffing up my knees and elbows. Andre and Mark giving me props for showing so much hustle as Shawn keeps up with the shit-talking, the scoring, the two of us high-fiving after each bucket. Four games later we're still undefeated, which is when the older guys call it a wrap.

I was just getting started, my brother says as his friends lean against the sagging gate, winded, chugging down a Gatorade each.

I gotta get home and ice these knees, Mark tells us, cracking us up as he hobbles off the court, exaggerating, or maybe not.

See you next week? Mark yells over from his car, before ducking in.

You already know it, Shawn says.

Still huffing and catching his breath, Andre sticks around. Unlacing his shoes and massaging his ankles, he watches as me and my brother put up more shots, keeping our bodies warm and loose. We're feeling ourselves after our four straight wins.

Your brother mentioned you like to play, Andre tells me, but he didn't say anything about how scrappy you are.

Couldn't touch the ball without you being in my face, he says, smiling and shaking his head, standing on his feet as Shawn starts up again, running up and down the court, working on his game as if he hasn't yet proven himself.

Back when I was your brother's age—he points at Shawn—believe me, I had even more energy than he does, Andre says. I wasn't the best but I was able to hold my own.

You went to UCLA? I ask him. It's my first time meeting someone in the Valley who went to a school that good. Over the hill in Westwood might as well be a different city from the L.A. I know.

Sure did. He nods, walking over to the open trunk of his silver Benz, dumping in his ball and sweaty clothes, throwing on a fresh tank top and coming back to the court.

His kind dark eyes look into mine. That hunger you've got in your step, Andre says, I'm telling you, don't let that go.

After an afternoon of pickup games, talking smack and dripping in sweat, is this the way it always goes for my brother? Getting to spend more time with his older friend, getting to hear about a past that doesn't seem so long ago even though Andre says it was. His body is lean and strong, his memories of when he was younger, playing the keys at different nightclubs, still come up from that place inside that I've seen other adults push away. They call their unfinished dreams just a bunch of fantasies as a way, I guess, to make it less painful, their regret less real. Because after a while I'm sure it gets old, carrying around this hunger all the time.

Though Andre doesn't claim that having a dream was naïve. Playing music was my first love, he says, always will be. And when I ask him how I find that for myself, worried that I never will, he stays quiet, running his hand over the black hair neatly trimmed on his chin and above his lip.

From how I've seen it, he says, you just gotta be patient. 'Cause if you're too hard on yourself you'll miss out on the thing that's been right in front of you, he tells me, his eyes sparking up again.

And maybe Shawn would say I'm crazy, but as Andre continues to share I can feel his younger self circling around us and chiming in, asking me to listen closely. Telling me that being young isn't something I have to give away, that the shine pouring out from his eyes . . . I have that, too, it's something I can keep, if I'm careful, no matter how old I get—

Giving your piano speech again? Shawn smirks, tossing his ball into Andre's chest. He bounces it right back.

Andre turns to me. Your brother always been a knuckle-head?

Pretty much.

I'm glad you came out today for some ball. It was nice to meet you, he says.

And after a quick handshake and hug, he and Shawn agree on plans to have lunch tomorrow in Woodland Hills, near Andre's office.

I watch as he cruises off in his Benz, wondering how good it must feel to have such a sweet ride, speeding onto Topanga, the wide street all to himself.

Seriously, I say to Shawn on our walk home, none of that bullshit where we start over 'cause you mess up your dribble. I'm drained, I tell him.

Man, he says, *cheer up*—did you forget we were the ones who went undefeated?

Some of us also had to work today, I remind him.

Well, it seemed like Andre was giving you some good advice, my brother says. But now you look all fucking depressed, he jokes, gently nudging his shoulder into mine.

I like him a lot, I tell Shawn. Probably the sweetest friend you have.

Shawn nods. He's hooking me up with a job at his real estate firm—did he mention that to you?

I shake my head.

I'll start as an assistant, but once I get licensed Andre says I'll be making some serious dough, my brother tells me. Looks like all those years of playing basketball is paying off.

Yeah. I nod. Maybe you're right, I tell him, staying quiet for the rest of our walk back, where at home, cleaning off my bloodied knees and sitting in the tub, I let the hot water fall over my face. After drying off, exhausted from the day, I thought I'd pass out as soon as I hit the bed but my mind keeps going.

Thinking about who it is I'm supposed to be, where to even begin.

The thing that's been right in front of you, Andre had said. It was one of those corny lines teachers and counselors love to hand out when offering their guidance, but hearing it come from him, watching it in his eyes, it had a different tone. So I try it, staring up at the ceiling, my eyes starting to burn with tears. *Please show me what's in front of me*, I keep repeating, like a prayer.

Driving through winding roads, roads I've never been on before, higher and higher we climb, outside long sheets of snow covering the mountains. Johnny's dad is at the wheel, visiting from Texas, making good on his promise.

Snowboarding, late night dinners by the fireplace. Whatever you boys want, his dad says, looking at Christian and me in the rearview mirror. The four of us are in the Suburban Cynthia let us use for the weekend, the whiskey on his dad's breath fills the car.

Music we haven't listened to before is coming through the speakers, CDs Johnny's dad brought with him from Houston, and I watch as he loses himself. Following along with the piano and the singer's deep beautiful voice, his dad belts out at the top of his lungs, eyes filling, red, singing along with a man he calls Withers—Johnny's dad doesn't miss a single beat, as though he's rehearsed for this exact moment. He turns to Johnny as his voice crackles with emotion, reminding his son that when things get hard, he can reach out. He keeps one hand on the steering wheel and the other around Johnny's shoulder. Just call on me, brother, he repeats over and again, smiling now. I pretend I know the song while nodding along, tapping on my knee to keep with the piano's tempo as I wait for it to happen.

I'm waiting for Johnny's dad to fade away, disappear. Because none of this is real, it can't be. We're listening to a song neither Christian nor me nor Johnny would ever listen to. But still, I can tell that Johnny's happy it's playing. For a moment he's getting to believe he has a dad who can be counted on, though the three of us know it isn't true. Johnny's dad comes around once a year, if that, and doesn't know the things Johnny goes through.

But the closer we get to the top, a cabin of our own awaiting us, the more real this late afternoon and the dipping sun becomes. Johnny's dad doesn't stop singing, doesn't disappear. You boys just wait, he tells us, nothing like gliding down on fresh powder.

And as he continues drumming against the steering wheel, Johnny doesn't say a word. He doesn't need to. He simply keeps nodding, his eyes straight ahead on the winding road like his dad's, the two of them with this special kind of bond they've somehow kept and built over the years. He glances over at his son every few minutes, as though Johnny's a member of his band or something, someone who's got even more talent than he does. Like they've jammed together before and they've got all these special gigs ahead of them. It's a kind of bond that goes deeper than just father and son, a bond me and my brothers know nothing of.

I hear the cabin's door creaking open, then gently shutting. I turn over toward the nightstand and the alarm clock's red digits say 3:13. Christian is asleep beside me on the pullout bed, and the twin next to ours, where Johnny was, is empty. On the couch his dad is passed out, snoring.

My neck and my knees and both of my ankles are throbbing, sore from our first day of snowboarding. Face-planting so many times on my way down the slope, I got to the point where my ears and nostrils were stuffed with snow. I was trying to keep up with Johnny. It was his first time and he was perfect, didn't fall once. Being a skater helps, he told me at the top of the hill, wearing an unbuttoned blue checkered flannel over his Astros jersey. When the sun was gone and the sky's fresh powder started falling—just as his dad had promised it would—soaring down the slope it looked as though Johnny had wings, both ends of his flannel catching in the wind while I did my best to stay close but couldn't. I didn't know how to slow down so each time I caught speed quickly I'd bail— I also didn't realize how much my hands would hurt without gloves. I plunged them into the snow whenever I fell and for the rest of the day my hands were numb, purple. Now the tiniest movement and it hurts like hell, the muscles in my legs are cramping, my neck is as stiff as concrete.

I turn over to fall back asleep, staying underneath the covers trying to relax my body   I can't.

The metal springs of the mattress squeak loud as I sit up, so I wait for a moment to make sure I don't wake Johnny's dad. Hanging from the chair beside him, he has his big puffy coat drying off. I borrow it for outside, going out in basketball shorts and his snow boots.

At a small playground down the hill from our cabin, I see the silhouette of Johnny's body on a swing, his head tilted up, breath streaming out. He turns to face me as I get closer, my feet crunching through the snow.

You good? I ask him.

Johnny's nose and cheeks are bright red, frosted snot above his lip. He's been crying and his eyes are soaked.

This *motherfucker*, he says, pointing toward the cabin, and already I know he's talking about his dad.

What he said to you on our drive here, I say, about calling more often?

Johnny nods. I used to beg him to come visit and now he's here talking this shit about calling if I'm ever in need, Johnny says, holding back his tears. Like some song can erase everything from the past as if I haven't needed him this entire time, Johnny tells me. He wipes the snot off his face.

Wanna know what he told me when we were on the lift? Johnny asks me, turning away.

He has another family in Houston, Johnny says. Two sons older than me. Every year blaming it on work—*I'm busy, Johnny, I'm busy*—the same stupid-ass lie whenever I'd tell him I wanted to see him.

Didn't even have the balls to tell it to me sober. He's been sucking from his flask ever since we left the Valley like it's a fucking tit. Johnny pushes off the ground, his body swaying on the swing as he leans as far back as he can without falling, his eyes closed.

How come your mom never told you? I ask him.

He shakes his head.

Said it would break her heart if he told her—so nah, she doesn't know and I'm not gonna say shit about it either.

Supposedly he's been waiting for me to *become a man* so he could tell me, Johnny says, lighting a cigarette.

I tell Johnny that my dad used to say the same thing to me. As if becoming a man is something special. And he knew it, too, I say, the way it'd make me smile back then, how much I loved hearing I was turning into one.

Now I just keep asking myself what the fuck's the point, 'cause it's here and I don't know what I'm supposed to do.

I look down at my own body, Baba probably wouldn't recognize me from the boy who left Iran over six years ago. Reaching almost six feet, with my shoulders widening, too, Maman claims my height comes from her father. My Baba-jan being so tall she says he had to tilt his head whenever entering their neighborhood's tiny mosque. And even the Adam's apple I always wanted . . . now it sticks out from my throat, my voice deep and rumbly.

Johnny stops his momentum and sits up straight on the swing, looking at me.

Have you heard from him? he asks.

I shake my head.

He probably wouldn't even recognize you now, Johnny says with a small smile on his lips.

Yeah he would, I tell him, reaching over as Johnny passes me his cigarette that's practically done. Though he probably wouldn't like what he'd see.

That's on him, Johnny says, and again he leans back on the swing, staring up at the stars blinking down at us.

'm working the drive-thru in early summer and the day is long and busy. Little kids are scarfing down Happy Meals then running around in the PlayPlace, the ball pit and plastic tunnels collecting vomit I have to then help clean up.

Daryl asked me to stay extra and I agreed even though I had plans to join Johnny and Shawn at home by the pool, swimming while Cynthia barbecues hot dogs and burgers.

Standing here in the back room, it's hot and cramped and I'm not allowed to sit, not even for a moment.

Not allowed to lean against the wall, it's not a good look for business, Daryl says, who works at his manager's desk from the back room, counting registers and tallying sheets, getting on calls with Corporate.

Car after car, the customers arrive, and my headset pings each time one pulls up to the drive-thru menu.

The orders don't change, not by much. Large Cokes and Big Macs, Happy Meals and Chicken McNuggets, though every once in a while someone will remember we carry baked apple pies, or they'll order a hot fudge sundae to go along with the two-for-one deal. I remind myself to do the same next time I'm on break.

One customer, before asking for the twenty-piece meal, tells me she and her friend heard that the chicken we use isn't real. After I tell them I wouldn't know anything about that, they order it anyways, asking for extra barbecue sauce and ranch.

Time crawls forward, sometimes even backward. I think it's been thirty minutes but it's actually been three, and then another customer, another ping in my headset.

I do as Daryl has asked and I sweep up the back room whenever there's a rare lull. He isn't watching over me and that's what I appreciate about him. He gives me my space and still he jumps in whenever I need a hand.

Daryl's the one who taught me how to sweep.

I told him it was pretty straightforward, doesn't everyone know to sweep? But it's not. There's an art to sweeping, Daryl likes to say.

First you take the broom, he showed me, sweeping the entire back room in one go. Then you bring in the dustpan, *after* you have your entire pile.

My headset pings, another customer.

I click on my microphone. Welcome to McDonald's.

We'll have twenty-two Big Macs, the customer yells.

There's a bunch of laughing in the background and it takes me a moment, but not long after I recognize the laugh as Johnny's.

Cynthia comes on. Hi, sweetie, she blurts out. We just came to say hello and to get some ice cream cones.

I stick my head out of the drive-thru window, and there she is in her silver Suburban, Johnny riding shotgun and Shawn in the back, waving.

When they pull up to the window I make sure my hat is

on straight. I stand a bit taller and I deepen my voice. I make sure to use all the tricks I learned from Daryl. How to be professional and polite, to leave a good impression.

Look at you, Cynthia says, handing me the money for the three ice cream cones. All grown up.

I start blushing and Johnny turns away, the look on his face is like it was when we were together in the tub, embarrassed, avoiding my eyes.

I tell them I'll see them at home after I'm off, and when Cynthia drives away, I turn to explain to Daryl who that was, but he's already smiling and nodding, leaning back in his leather chair with both palms around the back of his neck.

All of this, he says to me, his eyebrows lifted, gesturing not only to the back room but outside, too. One day it's gonna be a thing of your past, Daryl tells me, sitting back up in his chair. You do know that, right?

As I'm about to bury my hands into my pockets, which Daryl has told me plenty of times is unprofessional, I catch myself. I shrug, keeping my arms by my side, asking him what he means.

I've been here fourteen years and we hire young folks like you plenty of times, he tells me, give them a week, maybe two, and then it's no-call, no-show. They'd rather live on their mother's sofa than work. He chuckles, shaking his head. But you, he says, you've picked up on things quick and you've stuck with us. That's going to get you places.

We're told to keep our right hands over our hearts, not for only one but for many moments of silence, asked to silently pray for the Americans we've just lost. There are rumors that in New York you can smell the burnt flesh of those who've perished in the burning buildings, lost bodies trapped in the city's air.

We're gathered in the school's auditorium, where our principal's voice is raspy and strained as he tells us about the attacks. He looks confused as he stands on the stage in front of us, as though he's misplaced what he wants to say next. His big shaky hand slowly wipes away tears as they drip from his jowls. For a while he stands in silence, his head tilted down.

Carefully lifting his gaze to address our school, he stares straight into our nation's flag telling us it's okay to be angry, sad—it's normal to feel hatred boiling in our blood for the people who've caused this. All that means, Mr. Huffman says, is that we're deeply and truly American. He reminds us how lucky we are to be a part of this great and mighty land.

Sitting here with Steven and Danny, my friends from homeroom, I take a moment to look to my left and then my right—as I would at the end of namaz with Baba at mosque, whispering blessings to those sitting around us, our gentle greetings of peace—this time searching the faces of my classmates, wanting to know what being truly American looks like.

'Cause though I do my best to keep quiet as we were told to, for me it's different from what our principal is showing us. I'm not crying and don't feel scared, sitting still in my creaking wooden seat. Mr. Huffman up on the stage saying a big price will be paid, tears that won't stop falling from his pink puffy face . . . After all, we have the most powerful military in the world, he reminds us.

It isn't only him, though. Teachers, counselors and students, they look shocked, afraid—even the hardest-looking dudes are wiping away tears, their faces tightened. So that while everyone else is caught in our country's terror, afraid because they aren't sure whether or not we're safe, if al-Qaeda is planning another attack and if this time it will be L.A.—I sit here thinking about the day me and my brothers were taken to LAX, forced to board a plane. I had no idea where we'd end up, or if we'd even make it anywhere, felt like we would drop and crash into the ocean where Maman would never be able to find us, I'd never get to see home again. Only, for me and Justin and Shawn, when we did return, America never held moments of silence, didn't ask what had happened to us. How before Iran Justin used to be the one who would wake first, a small smile on his face, ready and dressed for school, setting an example I could look up to, one I no longer get to have. Where even though we've lived together, it feels like my brother was taken from me years ago, turned into someone alone, split into pieces, and even after reading so many books he hasn't been able to put himself back together.

As my friends lean in close from their seats, speaking loudly and proudly of the shit they're planning, how they'll take revenge on those who've caused this, still, I can't keep myself from remembering back.

Not until the end of the day at school do I realize that Steven and Danny see me, and anyone else who looks like me, daughters and sons of immigrants, Muslims, as the ones responsible for America's new grief, the ones who hijacked the planes and crashed them into the towers.

On my way home from work, I pause for a moment in front of the mosque Baba used to take me and my brothers to—standing here the way he would, stopping us before we entered through the parking lot for a lesson on how to live our lives—and see now there's the word *Sandniggers* tagged in big red letters on its walls, telling us to *Go back home*. From elementary school till now, every morning listening to the principal pledging allegiance over the intercom, I've made sure not to lean or slouch as I follow along with my classmates, reciting the words meant to make me feel proud of where I belong, of the home that we're told belongs to us, *One nation under God*—I've never seen it as or called America anything else but that, a big and beautiful house, ours.

My brother's the one who shows me what it looks like to have your heart broken. For two weeks straight Justin hasn't left our apartment, not since his girlfriend called things off a week before they were supposed to move in together, right after the New Year. He quit his job, said he couldn't stand spending time with her dad knowing he can't be with Vanessa, and yesterday morning I watched as he slammed his feet down onto his board, snapping it in half. Skating's a waste of time, he told me. But for him everything's become a waste of time. He doesn't read anymore, threw his books away, even Maman's copy of *Siddhartha*, which he used to say was the most important book he's ever read, now calling it a bunch of bullshit.

Justin stays in his bed until it's dark again, the blanket pulled over his face as if he's hiding from the world. Maman's tried to get him to leave the apartment, even offered on her day off to drive him to the library he loves, all the way downtown, and Shawn's tried, too. Inviting Justin to join him and Andre whenever they go out to eat. He's even let Justin know they're hiring at Champ's, that he can get him a job. But nothing's working, our brother says he isn't interested.

It's only late at night when he shows a bit of life. I hear Justin sobbing into his mattress, and I go into the kitchen to make his favorite meal, since these days he hardly ever eats.

Quesadillas with too much cheese stuffed inside, and to-night, as a special treat I added a scoopful of Maman's torshi on top. Justin's the only one who used to eat from her mas-sive supply of pickled vegetables. And he enjoyed it, too, eat-ing spoonful after spoonful by itself.

I bring the plate to his bed where he sits up with his pillow perched behind his neck, like a patient eating in a hospital room. I tell him we can stay up together talking while he eats, if he wants.

You've become quite the chef, he tells me, smiling an un-happy smile as he nibbles at the burnt edges of the tortilla.

Quesadilla plus Maman's torshi . . . I can't believe I didn't think of this myself, Justin says. After he's finished eating, I take the plate from his bed and keep it in my lap, and I listen. He tells me how special it was when he and Va-nessa went camping for his birthday, snuggled in front of the campfire.

That's the night I lost my virginity to her, Justin tells me, tears filling his eyes.

What was it like? I ask him.

Nirvana, he whispers, looking up at me. It was pure fuck-ing Nirvana. And I won't ever feel that way again, will I? my brother asks.

I want to tell him that that isn't true, but right now, with how hurt he is, he wouldn't really believe me.

I bet she's thinking the same about you, I say to Justin, it's not like those feelings just go away.

Maybe she got scared because of how fast the relationship was moving, I tell him.

Maybe it was her first time, too, I say, falling in love.

Yeah, he whispers, sitting up. Yeah I think you're right—I just need to give her time, Justin promises himself.

Then, coming out of his sadness, for a moment he turns to me—his dark eyes now strong and bright, the way I'm used to seeing them. You know you can always come to me for condoms, right? You don't have to share anything you don't feel comfortable telling me, Justin says. I just want to make sure my little bro is being safe.

Avoiding his eyes, I can feel my neck and face turning hot. I appreciate that, I tell my brother, who's the first in our family to speak to me about having sex. Maybe it's because he knows how I feel about Johnny. Maybe Justin's okay with it, me being the way I am.

And how they've shown it to us in porn, he tells me, I hope you know that isn't how it actually is. That's just a bunch of bullshit meant to keep people numbed out, as if bodies are meant only for fucking.

Real sex is nothing like that, Justin says.

Then what is it actually like? I ask my brother, surprising myself with my question, and him, too.

He lets out a big breath.

Man, now that's the million-dollar question, he tells me.

Well, he says, pausing, staring up at our bedroom ceiling.

When Vanessa and I would have sex, Justin starts, I wanted to show how deeply I feel for her, in a way that can't really be explained with words.

Try anyways, I say to him.

You're relentless. He chuckles, and again a pause, again letting out a deep breath.

We loved getting to explore each other's bodies, he tells

me. Seeing what felt good, what didn't, getting to learn new things about each other.

It should feel like you're having fun, not something you're forcing to happen. But no matter what, Justin says, now looking right into my eyes, whoever it is you end up choosing to be with, you need to show them that you care, that you respect them.

That you respect *all* of who they are, he adds, and that goes both ways.

I nod, wanting my brother to say more so that I can, too. Only now he's standing up from his bed, saying that's all the energy he has for tonight.

What happened to your earring by the way? I thought it looked good on you, I tell him.

Really? he says. I tossed it into the Wash after she and I broke up, but maybe I'll get a new one.

Walking across the room and carrying his plate to the kitchen, Justin shouts through the hallway saying it was my best quesadilla yet, which he says after each one, which makes me smile each time.

This is how I spend my winter break of senior year, staying up with Justin till the sun has already begun to break through the sky, even when I have the 7:00 A.M. breakfast shift at McDonald's. Listening to his stories of a broken heart, the things he's been through. Because even though he's hurting, bad, Justin's the one who's willing to show me what it looks like when you love.

On our way to Christian's party, Johnny and I stay on the paved path under the lights, avoiding the parts of Lanark Park we've learned to stay out of. Where from deep in the middle there's a sharp glow of cherry red, invisible hands passing around a blunt. Half shadows hang near the benches, the smell of weed snaking its way toward us. Let's cut through, Johnny suggests, breaking his own rule of taking the long way, but I trust he knows what he's doing. I follow him as he crosses into the baseball field, past the cracked and abandoned swimming pool, through the basketball courts that have been forgotten, too. The rims without nets, backboards all tagged up and the asphalt with chunks missing—I see now why Shawn hasn't been back since his first time coming, when we were kids, to practice his jump shot. I see why he prefers going to the church when he wants to hoop.

We exit Lanark and the house is right there. Across from the park and even before we get to the driveway you can hear the music blasting, floating from inside. It doesn't take long to recognize the beat, one of Dre's tracks from *2001*, the only album Christian's been listening to ever since it came out. With Snoop's voice looping through, stretchy and loose, you can't mistake it for another.

Inside are more shadowy faces I don't recognize, hot bodies bunched together, the living room damp with the smell of sweat. Most of the people here are older than Johnny, a few look like maybe they're my age, seniors in high school. When Christian sees us standing by the door, right away he starts shouting, yelling above the music.

Look who's here, he announces, one hand holding a blunt, the other a bottle of Jameson. He stumbles over, knocking into the side table. Johnny catches the lamp before it drops. Christian flings his body between us, his breath hot on my face, sour.

About time you grew up, Christian says into my ear as he points to a group of girls sitting on the sofa in the corner of the living room, talking and laughing and passing around a cigarette. I recognize Crystal from school.

Grabbing the bottle from Christian's hand, Johnny pours himself a shot. I watch as he tips his head back in one quick motion. I'm glad he doesn't ask me if I want to drink, glad he doesn't give the bottle back to Christian, either.

I'll be right back, Johnny tells me. When he leaves I wait a few minutes on my own, watching him as he nods at the people he knows, then hugging one of the girls from the sofa as she leaps up and hangs from his neck, kissing him on the cheek.

At first I stay by the table, where there's a bowl of soggy chips and salsa, then take a handful and go on my own, exploring the house, dark rooms followed by even darker ones, a backyard with a fire pit going. A group of guys stare me down through the sliding door's glass, the four of them with shaved heads. I recognize one of them from the Wash, tattoos on his neck snaking up his face, maybe he's the leader. I've seen them before, hanging around Lanark. They've never bothered me or my brothers, have always kept to themselves, but as Crystal walks up to me, her hand on my shoulder and passing me her cigarette, I can feel them watching me.

I'm glad you came, she says, standing close to my face. Her eyes have a glassy, glazed look to them. She's wearing black skinny jeans with a white tank top that hangs loose on her body, her flowery red bra showing through. Crystal's voice is soft and the dimples in her cheeks deep as she smiles at me, she's just as beautiful as she was the time we first met in Ms. Kim's classroom. Come join us, she says, pointing over to the sofa where Christian is now sitting, his girlfriend on his lap. He scoots over to make space, just enough room for one more body and I know he's setting it up that way on purpose. Situated so that Crystal would have to sit on my lap, the way Christian thinks I want her to.

Don't worry about them, she says, noticing my eyes look toward the guys outside, one of them still dogging me. He's just jealous he can't have me, she whispers as she leans in even closer, the smell of her hot skin turning me on as she wraps her arms around my neck.

I told Johnny I'd find him, I tell her, but I'll come back and join you guys. Which is when people start rushing through the sliding glass door to see what's happening outside, voices shouting louder and louder. Christian stands up from the sofa, shoves his way through the crowd as I follow behind.

In the side of the yard where it's dark there's a circle of three or four guys stomping on someone who's lying on the concrete, curled up and covering his face. As soon as I realize it's Johnny I push through to break up the fight and Christian grabs my shoulder. *Don't,* he tells me, they're jumping him in. I went through the same shit and it wasn't so bad, he says, a grin on his face. And when I shove Christian off me, the guy with tattoos on his face steps in front. If I were you, I'd listen to your homie, he says, looking me dead in the eyes.

I turn and leave the backyard, walking by Crystal as she asks me if everything's okay. Seeing Johnny like that, now there are tears coming up, and I don't know where to go or who to talk to, doing my best to keep myself from showing any emotion. I tell Crystal I have to leave.

Let me walk with you, she says, grabbing my hand.

Outside Crystal promises that Johnny's going to be fine, saying that he's been coming around for a while and that they're gonna go easy on him.

That's not the point, I tell her. He never told me anything about joining.

Didn't you know he already had? she asks me.

Starting a new war, our president's promise to end al-Qaeda in the Middle East is what finally gets my brother out of bed, bringing him back into himself. It's my higher power, Justin tells me, calling on him to serve.

All of those fucked up videos they keep playing on the internet, he says, people getting their heads chopped off—that shit has to stop.

So he starts to train, starting his days at dawn.

Before leaving for school, I climb up and sit on top of the brick wall surrounding our building's parking lot, and I watch as my brother gets himself ready to join the war. Wind sprints and crunches, push-ups and squats that never include any breaks, all while carrying a backpack full of textbooks.

It's hard seeing how much Justin pushes himself, all the blood in his body shooting up to his face as he heaves for air. Still, I know by being here we get to have our small window of time. After he's done, he joins me by the wall, showing me the different ways his body is changing, how excited he is for this new transformation.

And even though I don't agree with what he's doing, don't really believe he's actually going to join the army, that doesn't mean I don't look up to my brother. The way he sticks to things once his mind is made up, the way he understands things that nobody else does. He doesn't cut me off when I'm talking, doesn't tell me how I'm supposed to be. Justin listens, always, and sticks to his word when he said I can come to him about anything.

But about a month into his training, sometime around May, my brother changes again. More distant, to the point where I can't recognize him anymore. At night he no longer shares what he's going through, and he's lost more and more weight.

The last time Justin and I speak he's leaving our room and I block his way, telling him he needs to clean up his mess, which has spilled over to my side. And without any warning he throws me down on the floor, pinning me with his body. His neck is thick with veins and knotted as rope, and he yells straight into my eyes as he says for the last time that I need to learn about respect.

After that I ask Maman almost every day when she's going to make him move out. Because the way I see it—Justin's already gone. For all I care he can get shipped off to the war and never come back. It'd be one less body taking up space in our tiny apartment, one less person to be afraid of.

Waiting up for me after school, Danny leans against my locker taking pictures with his flip-phone of the cheerleaders walking past on their way to the bus, loading up for our school's away soccer game. He thinks they don't notice what he's doing, looking so dumb with Steven grinning beside him, his tongue licking around his fat lips.

Every Friday the three of us used to walk home together, stopping by the 7-Eleven on Sherman Way for a Slurpee and a bag of hot Cheetos, taking turns shoplifting a pack of Skittles just for the hell of it. Now that almost a year has passed since the attacks, I guess they've forgotten about it, how stupid it was blaming me for some shit I had nothing to do with.

Danny stands in front of me, blocking my way. His face is serious but he grins. I make room to reach for my locker dial by bumping through with my shoulder. I have a shift in an hour and if I'm late again Daryl's going to have to write me up.

What's the rush, Danny tells me. Does Osama have somewhere to be?

I thought by now you'd have some new jokes, I tell him as he hovers behind me, asking if it was my mom, or dad, who taught me how to make a bomb.

Taking out my textbook, I turn to face him and Steven, shutting my locker.

Did you guys forget we have a history test tomorrow? I say to them.

The origins of al-Qaeda. I heard there's gonna be an essay question on it, I tell Danny, and it sounds like you need to study up, little homie.

Danny steps closer to my face. I look down at him staring toward my chin. His breath smells of stale hot wings from lunch. So Osama likes to talk shit now, he says.

We're just messing around. Steven chuckles, stepping between us.

Are we though? Danny tells me, pushing him aside.

Sounds like this camel needs to be slapped straight, he says to me, knocking the textbook out from my hands. Even before I reach down to the ground to pick it up, in my head I already see what's going to happen next. He goes on talking shit about where I belong, pushing his crotch up against the top of my head as I get my textbook back from the ground. Standing up straight, I swing it hard across his face and hear the crunch of his nose underneath, though I was just aiming for his cheek, wanting him to feel how it is to be slapped, as he said I should be.

More blood than I thought a nose could carry comes rushing out, and he's shouting at me as he stumbles back, his hand cupped beneath his face catching the blood, as if he thinks he can shovel it back in.

I wait for Steven to do something, but he just stands beside Danny, stunned, switching between staring at the blood and at me.

Watch, motherfucker, Danny cries. You're going to pay for this, he tells me, tears rolling down his cheeks.

By the time I reach the end of the hallway, I start sprinting, about three miles from school to work and I run the whole way without stopping, my lungs empty and dry so that all throughout my shift, each time I breathe in, I cough up what tastes like metal.

At night when the knock comes, I already know it's him, probably with a friend, making true on his promise to get his revenge. We're in our room, Justin up in his bed with his CD player on as I get some homework done, and my chest starts beating so hard that its noise is all I can feel in my ears. So when Maman walks in saying someone's at the door, I don't actually hear what she's telling me and it's hard to walk straight without feeling dizzy.

Danny's staring down at the carpeted floor, his nose covered in bandage and stuffed with cotton as his mom stands beside him.

This is what your son did, she says, not looking at me but straight into Maman's face, gesturing toward Danny's nose. Lucky he didn't need surgery, but the doctor had to fix his *broken* nose, she tells Maman, emphasizing how hard I must've hit him to cause the bone in his nose to shift out of its place.

But Ms. Garcia herself has said it before, that I'm a good kid. She's watched Danny and me getting our schoolwork done together. Once she even pulled me aside in their kitchen to tell me what a good influence I'd been on him.

We don't have insurance and I have a bill waiting for me at the hospital, she continues, for eighteen hundred dollars.

You can pay now, Ms. Garcia says, raising her voice, or I'll have to press charges if that's—

Maman doesn't wait for her to finish. She steps away from the door to grab her purse, pulls out her checkbook, the same folded blue book I saw her use at the bank yesterday when balancing her account.

I watch Danny stare at the floor as Maman writes down the numbers, using the inside of the doorway to write against. It happens so quickly but at the same time it feels like the four of us are frozen in this moment, Maman signing her name at the bottom of the check, tearing it out as she hands it to his mom. And when Ms. Garcia asks if there's anything I have to say for myself, I wonder why the fuck *I* have to apologize.

I wait for Danny to speak up but he just keeps his head tilted down. And by the time he and his mom walk away, Maman has already left the door, leaving it to me to decide whether I'll come back in, to explain to Justin what just happened, or stay here outside our apartment in the hallway, on my own, thinking about the mornings I've heard Maman's alarm clock ringing, listening as she got up from the living room floor, folding the sheets and blanket, leaving in the dark for her shift at the hospital.

Eighteen hundred dollars. Maman wouldn't even look at me as she wrote out the check, upset, once again, at how much it costs to have me as her son.

Early in the evening there's a line of cars on Sherman Way waiting to turn into the parking lot. I cross to the other side of the street, not having planned on being here but I stay anyways, sitting on the pavement against the cinder-block wall. Fathers and their sons and a few elderly Muslims move inside for Maghrib prayer, bunched together while scattered groups of women wait for them to enter before ducking in through a separate entrance around the back.

Khoda's house is your house, too, Baba used to tell us, and I walk up the short staircase leading to the entrance, wanting to see, even if for a brief moment, what it feels like to be back inside the mosque.

A small crowd gathers as everyone removes their shoes and greetings of As salaam alaikum float through the hushed and narrow hallways. After being broken into and trashed, the inside of the mosque has been remodeled, now clean and spacious, without that old musty smell from when I was a kid.

Coming from the kitchen I spot the imam, he's holding a large silver tray offering tea and sweets. I take one of the small Styrofoam cups, along with a few dates. The imam looks into my eyes, calm and gentle, asking how I am doing, standing here as if he has all the time in the world and it feels like I'm back in Haji Agha's garden sitting across from my grandfather and Agha Zadeh. It's as though the imam knows who I am, even if he doesn't recognize me from before. How could he? I'm not a little kid anymore, being ushered in by Baba. My chin and cheeks have thick black hair because I haven't shaved, letting my beard grow out.

Sipping my tea and watching the elders go into the back room for wudu, I decide I'm going to join them in prayer, try to talk to God.

In the washroom I take an open seat between a father and his boy, running my feet underneath the faucet and washing between my toes, splashing my arms and my face, the water cold and refreshing. The imam's call to prayer echoes throughout the small building. I join the men in the mosque's main room.

With my toes up against the line marked in the dark green carpet, I stand with my arms straight down by my sides, a few feet behind the imam who's taken his place in the mihrab up front. The man standing to my right taps me on my shoulder, his eyes dark and polite, he reminds me that we're inside a mosque that belongs to Sunnis. And for God to accept your prayer, you must do it like this, the man whispers and shows me, folding his arms across his chest, with his head tilted down. Showing him that for me it doesn't matter, whether the mosque accepts me or not, I keep my arms where they are, by my sides, my face tilted up toward God.

Bismillah hir rahman nir rahim, the imam begins, and it's still with me, the opening surah of the Qur'an that Baba helped us memorize as kids. I follow along, softly singing the verses as the sounds of Arabic move through my chest and up into my throat, reverberating throughout my body.

And it isn't so much that I care for the meaning that's behind the prayer, what the Arabic words actually mean, or if God rejects my prayer because like the man said I'm not doing it correctly. I continue because of the way the verses make me feel, no longer afraid or wanting to hide, remembering now that there's always been more to me than the white American boy I've wanted so badly to be, and look like. Ever since the attacks I've stopped praying, pretending that namaz—its stillness and movement, the quiet I feel from connecting with God and the love I feel toward the country my parents come from—I've pretended as though these things were never here, didn't exist. But sung by the imam in his strong and sorrowful voice, the sounds of these ancient words bring me back, like that beautiful bridge Khaleh walked me and my brothers across in Isfahan, leading me to this part of my past I tried so hard to erase. Because this part of myself *is* being American, at least for me, and from now on I'm going to protect it, cherish it, sing it each night before falling asleep— this sacred language that my grandfather and his grandfather before him turned to when they looked up to God with their palms held out, open, ready to receive whatever blessing would come.

Shawn shakes me awake, pressing the phone receiver into my chest, he says Baba's on the phone.

It's dark outside and I can't tell whether I've slept through the night, after falling asleep on the sofa when I got home from school after my finals, or if it was just a nap.

What? What time is it? I ask him.

It's Baba, Shawn says with a look on his face I haven't seen in years.

Why the hell would he call now? I ask my brother, not knowing if Shawn's trying to play one of his stupid pranks on me.

But my brother's face is serious. C'mon, he says, get up.

I don't move, closing my eyes again. I tell Shawn to leave me alone.

He wants to talk to you, my brother says, dropping the cordless phone onto my chest.

He then reaches over, holding his hand open for me to grab, and pulls me up from the sofa.

I sit for a second with my feet on the ground, my head pounding, the phone in my lap.

What does he want? I ask my brother, who stays here, standing over me, telling me to just pick it up, that it isn't going to kill me.

Listening as Baba breathes into the receiver, heavy and slow, I wait.

He says my name, repeating it over and over.

I'm here, I finally tell him.

Chetori, he asks, how are you?

It's been almost eight years since I've heard Baba's voice, and I thought he would sound different to me, like someone I wouldn't be able to recognize, at least that's what I hoped for.

But he sounds just as I remember him, as if we've been frozen in time together. His voice is weak and then strong, sad and then scary, shifting so quickly between each moment that as I listen to him it's hard, maybe impossible, to settle on any one feeling for longer than a few seconds, like how it was when I was little and I'd be with him.

I've missed you, Baba says, as I stay quiet.

I've thought about you every single day since you left me, he says.

I'm coming back and I want you at LAX when I land, Baba then tells me, his voice serious.

I stand up from the sofa and shove the phone into my brother's chest. He tosses it right back at me, telling me he already spoke to Baba, that it's my turn and to at least give him a chance to finish.

Are you there? Baba asks as I put the phone back to my ear.

Pesaram, he whispers, sniffling into the phone, my boy, my—

Favorite, I say to him, the word jumping out of my throat.

Yes, he continues, saying how good it is to hear my voice, how happy he is to know he'll get to see me again.

When I don't say anything back, Baba lays out a list of what he wants, what he expects when he arrives at the airport, making his voice harsh and strong, like he used to back when he was our dad.

Not a day has gone by, he tells me, that he hasn't regretted letting me and my brothers leave with that whore, which is what he calls my aunt. And now something beneath my skin fires up, and if Shawn wasn't still standing over me in the dark, his thick body intimidating me, I'd have told my dad to go fuck himself. I'm reminded of why I hoped to never hear from Baba again, wanting to forget that he's still alive, his heavy breath. He tells me about his one and only wish, for us to be a family again, his voice cracking, as though being a father is a fucking performance, trying to get his son to believe in his sadness.

When are you coming back? I ask, saying it quick, hard.

I'll be there for Nowruz, he tells me, a smile on his face which I can feel through the line. The five of us together, Baba says, just as it was before. Do you remember how we used to drive through Malibu's canyon, he says, all the way to the water?

Iran just isn't the same anymore, he goes on, his voice now soft and tired, telling me why he's coming back after eight years, when the truth probably has something to do with the fact that Amoo won't budge, isn't going to close his school and sell the building, won't let himself be bullied by his older brother.

The world has changed, pesaram, there's nothing here for me. I'm going to rebuild my life where it belongs, Baba says, hoping America will give him another chance, happy to welcome back my dad who once swore he was the greatest engineer to ever come from Iran.

Agha Mohandes, that's the name the neighbors next to Haji Agha's would call Baba by, *Mr. Engineer*. And each time we were together he would smile proudly and pat me on the head, asking me to pay close attention and to remember what it looked like when a man was respected all across the globe.

Remember, he says, you only get one father in this life, and that a father must be with his sons.

As I hold the phone to my ear, listening to him, I know this will be the last time I hear Baba's voice, and it makes me feel pathetic that part of me misses him, knowing I won't ever see my dad again.

I know I can count on you, Baba tells me, now whispering into the phone as if he's trying to place his mouth right beside my ear.

I'll see you at LAX, he says.

Take care, Baba, is all I'm able to say, setting down the phone.

When Johnny answers the door, pretending I don't notice his busted lip, I ask, Your mom working tonight?

Yup, he nods.

Grab your hoodie, then, I say. By the time he asks where we're going, I'm already halfway down the hallway. I'll meet you out front, I tell him.

Pacing back and forth outside, when Johnny walks through the gate I dig into my pockets, holding out my closed fist, then drop change into his palm. Your early birthday present, I tell him. For the bus.

I lead the way and Johnny follows behind as we walk to the corner of Sherman Way and Topanga. There's a seat between two people waiting at the stop, but neither of us take it, instead taking turns to step out onto the street, looking for the bus.

I ask him about it, pointing to his lip, the cut above his eye. I want to hear it from Johnny, the rest of the story from the night he got jumped.

It's worse than it looks, he says, forcing a smile and picking at the crusted scab forming over the cut. You should've seen Christian. He laughs. They fucked him up pretty good.

The bus is now pulling up to the curb. Where we going? he asks.

Stoney Point, I tell him, in Chatsworth. Justin's been telling me about it for a while now. Says at night you can see a bunch of stars, all those constellations we used to learn about in school.

Dope. Johnny nods. He shows me the grin on his face, rubbing it in. He wants me to admit he was right, back when I used to be afraid of the bus. No crackheads, no horny dudes looking to fuck, nobody here who's going to bother us.

And after dropping the coins into the slot, I follow him down the aisle, passing a woman sitting alone, balancing groceries on her lap, and a younger girl a few rows behind, using the empty seat to put up her legs. A CD player is clutched in her hands, black headphones over her ears.

In the very back I take the seat against the window, Johnny's body tucked against mine. As soon as the doors are sealed shut and the lights switch off, with the bus humming forward, I place my hand inside the pocket of his hoodie. I let the warmth of his lap move through my palm, into my arm and down through my stomach. With his hand now resting on top of my thigh, I stare from behind the tall wide window as streetlights flare up the misty rain sprinkling through the night.

I watch as it all sweeps by and us along with it. I bury my hand into Johnny's. Like this, I think to myself, I don't want the bus to make it to our stop. The entire night to ourselves riding wherever, doesn't matter where.

I turn away from the window and tell Johnny about the call with Baba, how he's coming back from Iran.

Your mom's not gonna let him move back in, he asks, is she?

I shake my head. I don't think so, I tell him, again looking out the window watching the soft rain.

Maybe because I've been afraid things would end up the way they did with Justin and his girlfriend, that we'd break apart, leaving behind the most precious parts of ourselves . . . Maybe that's why I've never told Johnny about Baba and me.

But I do, telling him about the night in Isfahan at Haji Agha's house, when Baba joined me underneath the covers, covering my eyes and peeling down my pants. As I explain the things he did, I wait for Johnny to cut me off, to say it's too much—but he doesn't. Instead he listens, moving his hand away from my thigh, no longer slouching in his seat. He sits up straight, his body stiffening. My voice cracking, tears begin to fall gently like the rain outside.

I turn toward Johnny, looking right into his eyes, asking myself why I ever believed that what happened with Baba and me wasn't something I could share with him.

Shawn and Justin too? he asks, his voice low.

No, I tell him, remembering how Baba would whisper it into my ear, that I was his favorite, and that it was only for us to know.

Between us there's now just the quiet hum of the bus. Johnny shoots up from his seat, reaches over to pull the yellow cord running along the edges of the window.

This isn't our stop, I tell him, and before I can say anything else the bus is already pulling against the curb, Johnny moving toward the door.

One step down the exit, he looks over his shoulder and sees I'm not behind him, his hand pushing the door open.

He walks back to our seat and reaches out for my hand.

We're good, he says. Come on.

Johnny marches up the wet, yellow-lit street, and I follow behind. The rain hitting my face feels right. Johnny picks up his pace, it's hard for me to keep up. Suddenly he stops and when he turns around, he puts his palm against my chest, softly. There's a trail of clear snot running down his nose.

Listen, Johnny tells me, searching for the right words to say before continuing. The things Baba did to me, he says he wishes he could take them away, all of it. And I can hear it in his splintered voice, how he's known that something was wrong, has been wrong for a very long time, just never knew what to say.

We don't have to go to Stoney Point anymore if you don't want to, I tell him.

It's up to you, he says, wiping his nose and the rain off his cheeks.

Let's keep going, I tell him. We can walk the rest of the way.

All right. He nods.

Walking up Topanga, again Johnny pauses, turning to me. We're going to make sure he never gets to touch you again, he tells me. You know that, right?

Yeah, I tell Johnny, that's my plan. I bring his body closer to mine so I can put my hand inside the pocket of his hoodie, which I do, linking his cold fingers into my own.

oday Justin leaves for Fort Benning, Georgia, where
he's chosen to go because not only will he get to complete his basic training but combat training as well. He
double-checks our room, making sure he didn't leave anything important behind. His army-green duffel bag with our
last name stitched on its side, a gift from Shawn, is stuffed
with only essentials.

Maman is by the door with the keys in her hand, looking
to the side. Shawn's eyes are filling, telling me how proud he
is of our brother. He's got some serious fucking cojones, he
says. Shawn likes to think he's some kind of pro with Spanish, as though it were his first language, not Farsi.

As Justin walks out from our room, I can't bring myself
to look him in his eyes. Instead I stare at our name on his
bag.

Aren't they going to say you're with them? I ask my
brother, pointing down.

With who?

Terrorists, I say.

I dare them to, Justin quickly responds. The way he says
it, his voice strong and hard, his gaze serious, I can tell he
means it. That whether it's in boot camp or once he's in combat, regardless of what side it comes from, if somebody ac-

cuses him of being a terrorist, he's going to make sure they never call him that again.

Justin's got on the same black high-top boots he's worn every morning in the parking lot while training, and he tells us he's never felt better. His head is clear, he isn't afraid, he says he knows what his purpose is.

One more thing, Maman announces, closing the front door right after opening it, and Justin sighs, his face melting into a smile. I already told you, he tells Maman, I can't fit anything else in my bag.

From the freezer our mom takes out a Tupperware of koo-koo sabzi she made just for him, then unzips his duffel bag and places it inside. For when you get hungry, Maman tells him. And how is he supposed to say no to that?

At the door Shawn gives Justin the hardest hug I've ever seen from my brother, even kissing him on both cheeks, the way Khaleh did when she said bye to us at the airport in Teh-ran. Take care of yourself, he tells Justin, who picks up his duffel bag once more and stands there, waiting for me.

I walk over from the kitchen, trying not to think about what's going to happen to my brother. Right now he's smil-ing, his eyes soft, I focus on that instead.

Doesn't matter where you end up, he tells me. As soon as I'm allowed, I'm going to come visit you, Justin says, open-ing the door and shutting it behind him one last time.

When I get home from work that night, taking off my shoes at the door, again there's the stale smell that makes its way from my sweaty feet, spreading throughout our apartment.

You for sure have athlete's foot, Shawn's warned me, but the clinic on Sherman Way, where as kids we went for our shots for school, it's impossible to get an appointment that isn't months away, so I haven't bothered.

Using the collar of her shirt to cover her nose, Maman walks out from the bathroom. Toro Khoda, she tells me, pointing down at my shoes, get *rid* of them.

She goes to open the living room window, and she won't stop trying to clear out the air in front of her nose, using her hand as a fan, making me laugh so hard. *Peeeeeef,* she keeps blurting out from beneath her shirt, the same reaction she has whenever Shawn goozes in front of us, for us to smell *for our enjoyment* he's always saying after ripping one of his loud and long nasty farts, making sure to leave only once his masterpiece is complete.

Now Maman pulls a glass from the living room's wooden cabinet, and pours herself a chai from the stove even though it's almost midnight.

She takes a seat on the sofa, a photo album open out on her lap. This is my favorite one, Maman says, holding up a photo of Justin sitting with his legs crossed on the floor in the den at our old house, small towers of Legos spread around him. Smiling big for Baba's camera, the flash shining on my brother's pink gums and tiny white teeth, dimples stamped in both of his cheeks.

He looks so happy, I tell her.

As a kid was he always like this? I ask, and Maman nods. Even as a newborn, she tells me, your brother was so calm and gentle.

I wish I was there to have seen that, I tell her, setting the photo aside on the coffee table and holding out my hand for her. It's been a long day, Maman. Let's call it a night.

She waves away my hand and says she isn't tired. Then she tells me she misses having my brother around the apartment, and I don't mean to, but it makes me laugh. It was only this morning that he left, I remind her.

And anyways, I say to her, when he was here it's not like you guys talked.

Doesn't matter, she tells me. He lived in this apartment, she says, didn't he?

Maman takes the picture from the coffee table. Help me frame this and hang it on the wall, she says, pointing toward the hallway.

I promise her that I'll do it tomorrow.

That's what you tell me but then you forget. She shakes her head, standing and walking to the kitchen counter, where she switches on her small radio. The only station she listens to, 670 AM, is a nonstop mix of Iranian journalists and doctors and lawyers discussing current events, the war in the Middle East. I remove a photograph of her and Khaleh that's wedged between the album's sticky pages. I hold it up for her to see. When was this taken? I ask, my voice soft over the radio's loud volume.

That? Maman sighs.

I don't remember exactly when, she says, now taking a seat beside me on the sofa. But it was when Khaleh still lived in Isfahan. Look how young we were. She smiles.

Maman and her sister, standing together on the Khaju Bridge, just as me and my brothers did with our aunt, hundreds of Isfahanis around us sitting on the park's grass. I loved listening to the voices of accented Farsi, so soft and sweet and easy, filling the empty riverbed below. And now whenever asked, I remember feeling that me and my brothers could say we belonged to a place, could tell our friends in the Valley where our family comes from—what Iran sounds and looks and smells like—of the private sorrow they've had to bury deep into their country's soil, that it's a part of who we are. Carrying inside us not only Iran's long history of beauty and art but its darkness, too.

Don't let it get ruined, Maman tells me, pointing down at my hands, my greasy fingertips blotting the picture.

How come you've never asked what it was like for us in Iran?

She leans back into the corner of the sofa, holding on to her glass of chai with both hands in her lap. And while her eyes are still with mine I wait for her to say something, to explain, but she doesn't. Instead turning her face away, she stares toward the living room's dark window and watches the reflection of us sitting together—but maybe not. Maybe what Maman is choosing to look at is different from the way I see us, me looking toward her, close, wanting her to talk.

But it stretches on, the quiet between Maman and me growing deeper, and it pushes me further, feels like I'm back in that room at Haji Agha's where I would whisper for her, stuck, where she couldn't hear me, wouldn't show up. I set the picture onto her lap.

After a moment Maman looks down, then up at me, her eyes wet and red, a little less far away.

When Khaleh took us to the bridge, I begin again, starting

since Maman won't, she said the two of you used to go there together all the time.

Maman nods to herself, then leans forward and sets her glass of tea onto the coffee table. I remember, she says, turning to face me as I wait for her words to catch up to her tongue.

Very late at night Khaleh would take me to go sit by the river—and it wasn't empty the way it is now, Maman says. The river used to be full. We had fish and plants and fresh water, it was so beautiful, Maman tells me. It was our favorite place to go.

Khaleh must have told you how she learned to drive, Maman asks me.

Naa, I tell her.

Yavashaki, once Baba-jan was asleep, she would sneak into his car and practice. Driving with no permit or license, Maman says, letting out a quick but loud laugh. Can you believe that?

Didn't he catch her though? I say. Khaleh told me one night he stayed by the door until she got home, waiting for her with a big-ass branch he picked from the backyard.

Maman nods. That didn't stop her from doing it again, she tells me. And when he tried to set her up for marriage, Maman says, I was the only person who knew she was going to leave. At first I didn't believe her, she was eighteen, why didn't she want to get married?

So that's why Khaleh lives in Tehran? I ask. She left because of Baba-jan?

Areh, Maman nods. And for years she didn't come back to visit, not until she heard I was marrying your baba.

For Nowruz, I tell Maman, when he comes back, you know I'm not gonna be here, right?

She neither nods nor shakes her head, but her eyes begin to fill, letting me know she understands what I'm telling her.

Tears fall from her face onto the photograph she's still holding in her lap. For the first time Maman allows herself to cry in front of me, hard, covering her mouth with the back of her hand.

I stay quiet, listening to our past, which now sits between us. Maman's face is covered in sadness as she breaks into herself. She shows her pain to me, the closest it's ever felt. And as Maman uses her heart to crack open the night, in this in-between of nothing—no more words or questions, no arguing or shouting that she's going to force me to stay— she shows me she's known it herself, that what I feel isn't wrong. She can't replace what's been taken from me, and lost. There's more for me, of course there is, but not here.

At first it's hard to recognize his voice, as if it's deeper, more grown since the last time I saw him, almost two months ago. My brother says that once he's finished with boot camp in a few weeks, he'll be starting another phase of training, this one more advanced.

I got recruited for Special Forces, he tells me, his voice proud over the phone as he explains what that means, the small prestigious squad he'll be a part of, deployed to Afghanistan in less than a year.

Aren't there other jobs you can take on? I ask. You've always been so good with math and science.

Yeah but this is what I want, he tells me.

So you can get killed? I want to ask. 'Cause based on what we've been hearing about the war, each day the death toll is rising, hospitals and markets getting bombed. Chances are my brother will get shot, or step on a land mine, leaving leftover pieces of his body we'll have to identify. I want to know what Justin's eyes look like now that he's been away from home. I wonder how they've changed, if they have. I want to know what he looks like with his army haircut, and if he was sad to lose his long black hair.

He fills me in some more on how it's been in boot camp. The platoon he's been assigned to, and how he feels like he's the strongest one—in fact he *knows* he is because out of all the recruits he scored the highest on the physical exam, impressing even his drill sergeant with his near-perfect score. Justin says he feels as if this has been his calling all along, something he was prepared for, pushing his mind and his body long before he arrived at boot camp, how happy he is that he's found a way to make that useful.

Just another minute, he says to a voice nearby, away from the phone. Then announcing out loud, making sure the person from his platoon that's rushing him backs off, he tells me, We get an hour between us and these guys love hogging it all to themselves. This is the first time he's made a call, he says, they can wait.

I need to get out of the Valley, I tell him, hoping he'll change his mind about going into combat, maybe he'll want to join me after his service is done. I hope you aren't joking, he tells me, his voice excited, smiling through the phone and I can hear him pacing around now, wherever he is.

You need me to spot you? he asks me. I've got some money coming my way for enlisting, he says. Give me the information to your account and I'll wire you some money to help out.

I've saved up a good amount from work, I tell him. I'll be fine.

Now that I have his full attention again, I ask my brother if he remembers that night in the kitchen when I joined him after he got home from that big party, when he first told me about Vanessa.

He fumbles with the phone, bringing it close to his mouth. Yeah, of course, he says.

Why do you ask?

I've never forgotten it, I say. You had this beautiful look in your eyes, it was as if every part of you was glowing because you had fallen in love.

Do you think it'll happen for me, getting to feel something like that? I ask my brother.

Justin doesn't say anything, he stays quiet, his quiet that says maybe I've brought up bad memories for him.

He sighs into the phone.

That glow you think you saw in my eyes, Justin tells me, that's *yours*, bro. I even remember being jealous of it, he says. When we were little, the way Johnny and Cynthia, Maman, whoever . . . how they'd always have smiles on their faces whenever they'd see you, always wanting you to be around them.

If you're going to leave, he says to me, it needs to be because that's what *you* want, and not because you're running away. You start running now and I promise you, Justin says, you'll be running the rest of your life.

Do you understand what I'm saying?

I think so, I tell him, as I hear laughter in the background.

Listen, these guys won't stop bugging me, he says. I'm gonna get off now so they shut up.

Before Justin goes I ask if he'll write and let me know when he's going to be deployed.

He promises he will, both of us are quiet on the phone for a moment, and then another, until finally Justin hangs up.

Christmas looks a little different this year. The temperature drops by like twenty degrees, a break from the sun and its heat. It's not even four o'clock yet and already the day has felt long, not much for me to do. Earlier this morning Maman left for her shift at the hospital, a double. Usually I'd be at Cynthia's by now, enjoying her holiday special, arroz con gandules, but this year Johnny said not to bother coming by, he'd be with Christian somewhere else.

It's not as though we celebrated together before, gathering for the holidays like so many families do, but that doesn't make being alone any easier. Which is why I can't stay in our apartment anymore, lying on the sofa alone pretending to be asleep.

So I walk over to Lanark, making sure to stay on the sidewalk that circles around in a big loop, lit by the orange lamps. I pause at each corner, looking in from the outside. The playground is still, no barbecues going or music playing, the park is empty. I brought my basketball shoes in my backpack just in case. Maybe at the court where Shawn goes after work there are some of the guys running pickup games, before getting ready for their big feast.

Walking to the abandoned church and dribbling the ball between my legs, nowhere near as good as my brother is but still, the thump of the rubber hitting the concrete comforts me, a familiar sound.

But it was dumb to have thought people would be out in the cold playing at the court. Nobody is here, everyone inside their homes.

In the apartments on the opposite side of the church, I watch as a family gathers in their living room, their blinds up and every light switched on, making it easy to see, to watch as they set their long dinner table. It's the time of year, as Christian used to say, when every tia and tio comes around—all gathered by the big lit Christmas tree, the table set with sparkling silverware and fancy plates, a huge ham in the middle.

I lie down on the pavement at half court, my arms and legs stretched out like Johnny's dad had showed us when he made angels outside of our cabin in the snow. I breathe out small white clouds in front of my mouth, watch them disappear.

Thing is, though, even if my family wanted to spend time with me I wouldn't want to be around them, wouldn't know what to say. I want a different family, a new one—

Fuck this place, I shout, standing to my feet. I chuck Shawn's Spalding at the rim as hard as I can, letting it ricochet to wherever it ends up.

leave this place the same way Baba once took me and my brothers. I take the bus to LAX, exiting at the terminal, and I remember how massive this airport felt. Like a city of its own. And how is it that in my body I can still feel that night we were brought here, the three of us sleepy-eyed, confused, yet wanting so badly to stay. This time, it's me who gets to decide. And I'm not leaving because Baba is coming back— I'm going because I need to figure out where I belong. It was in New York where my dad had his chance to be young, and free. I want to know what that feels like. Not just for myself, but to share it, to live young with those around me.

I have with me the small rolling suitcase I found shoved in the back of the closet, what I came home with from Iran. Now it's packed with my nonslip work shoes, T-shirts and jeans, a big puffy blue jacket Johnny insisted that I take.

I could have gone on a Greyhound, much cheaper and much easier, but I worried I'd get off somewhere in between L.A. and New York, scared of what I'm doing. But getting on a plane, a straight flight, I wouldn't have the choice but to arrive. I know this is what I have to do for my life to become mine, to become something real. Finally I'll get to see, and have, what before only lived inside of me—this constant hum of color and dreams, of wanting more, always more than the life I was shown in the Valley.

Inside the terminal passengers stand and wait, the line to enter the gate is backed up, bodies wrapping around in a maze. Airport security so different from the last time I was here, but the last time I was here the Twin Towers were still reaching into the sky.

I take my place in line, boarding pass in hand. My knees feel like they're going to lock into themselves. My heart is beating hard. When I was little, in the car on our way to some stranger's house somewhere deep in the Valley, someone from the mosque who agreed to host weekly Qur'an gatherings, Baba asked if I had decided what I would be when I grew up. His question surprised me, the way he'd expected an answer right away, as if he'd been showing me how to decide who I want to become, how to find what I love all along. I had no idea then, I still don't. The only thing that stuck with me is what came from being in Ms. Kim's classroom, watching the way she carefully recited each word during our weekly spelling bees. It didn't matter what the word was, how simple, the way she'd stand up and speak loud into the classroom as we all stayed quiet made it feel as if all words are holy. Maybe Khaleh felt that way, too. Maybe that's the reason she asked Maman to give me Forough's book before I left. Running her fingers over a folded-down page, the pretty script of swirls and dots, Maman read the words for me—*I will greet the sun again, the stream that once flowed in me . . . I will come, I will come, I will come and the entrance will be filled with love.* They were the sounds of something so pure, Forough's desires as strong as this hunger I feel inside, promising me more and then more, more heat as its light comes through—I feel it now, pushing me on.

Next, the officer announces, loud.

I step forward.

I hand the woman my school ID and boarding pass, forcing a smile the same way I forced myself to smile into the camera on my first day of senior year when the photo was taken.

She spends longer than usual looking at my ID and then calls over to her coworker, or maybe it's her supervisor. His uniform is a different color than her blue. He, too, takes his time looking over my pass and ID, holding up the line behind me.

Your name on your boarding pass doesn't match what's on your ID, he finally says.

What's your full name? he asks in a voice that didn't start here in L.A., an accent from a part of America I'll probably never visit. I mumble an answer and pull out my passport.

He looks it over, turning it around, front and back, then again up at me, his soft blue eyes fixed on my face, as if he's scanning for something in my eyes and facial hair.

How do you say your first name, son?

The question knocks me back.

Holding the officer's gaze, I answer.

My name, all of it, fills my mouth, my chest.

The officer doesn't ask a second time and wishes me a safe flight. I walk toward the gate and say it again, over and over. I practice how it sounds, listen as it makes its way.

Acknowledgments

It was very unlikely for me to have arrived at this page, and were it not for you, dearest reader, I wouldn't have made it. So as we Iranians often say, dastetoon dard nakone—*thank you*, for offering me this special chance to be here—I pray your hands never tire, never know hurt.

And to the crew who made this production possible: the kind and generous folks who contributed much-needed funds for my MFA; Wendy S. Walters, who showed me what it means to feel, and to listen to every word on the page; Alice Quinn, who introduced me to poetry; Jodee Davis, who helped me remember; Heidi Julavits, whose writing workshop showed me that fiction could tell the truth; Martin Pousson, who responded swiftly and generously when I introduced myself via email back in 2015, direct from Oscar Wilde's native land, taking me under his wing; Hannah Shealy and the Shealy family, who showed me home; Guy Philip, my caffeine guru; Tara Grbovic, who showed me what it means to be an artist; Simon Toop and the extraordinary team at the Clegg Agency, and of course, he, himself, the ever-so-legendary Bill Clegg, who gave me a life to look forward to; Parisa Ebrahimi, who gave me time to write, and write, the chance to fall and fail and thrive—I don't think it's an exaggeration to say that together we rewrote this novel precisely 1,001 times; David Ebershoff, who kindly asked if there were more pages I could send, pages which changed my life; Isabel Wall, who listened and offered her guidance each time I called; the design, marketing, publicity and production team at Hogarth (Penguin Random House), who put forth such extraordinary work; Ojan Assadolahi, who's kept me in shape by keeping the laughter flowing; my two older brothers, whom I love dearly, from whom I learn each and every day, and my mother, oh, *Mami-joon—merci*, sending you each a million thanks and a thousand kisses, forever.

PHOTO: ARIANNA SHOOSHANI

Khashayar J. Khabushani was born in Van Nuys, California, in 1992. During his childhood he spent time in Iran before returning to Los Angeles. He studied philosophy at California State University, Northridge, and prior to completing his MFA at Columbia University, he worked as a middle school teacher. This is his first novel.

khashayarjkhabushani.com

About the Type

This book was set in Fournier, a typeface named for Pierre-Simon Fournier (1712–68), the youngest son of a French printing family. He started out engraving woodblocks and large capitals, then moved on to fonts of type. In 1736 he began his own foundry and made several important contributions in the field of type design; he is said to have cut 147 alphabets of his own creation. Fournier is probably best remembered as the designer of St. Augustine Ordinaire, a face that served as the model for the Monotype Corporation's Fournier, which was released in 1925.